名人故事×經濟策略×文學名著×法律思潮

一生必知的世界文化

英語導覽

一本書帶你從八個層面全方位掌握英語！

U0075111

莊琦春，
陸香，丁碩瑞　編著

掌握語音、文法、單字，就等於掌握了一門語言？
不了解文化背景，猶如只學了皮毛而無習得其精髓！

本書橫跨多個領域，英語和知識結合，
幫助讀者順利拓展交際活動！

特別收錄　**經典演講稿、散文名篇**

目錄

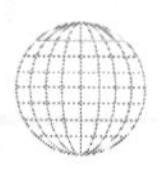

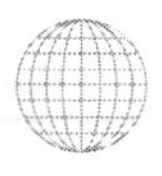

前言

對於外語學習的傳統看法是只要學會語音、語法和詞彙就算掌握了這門外語。近幾十年來，外語界對這個問題的看法發生了很大的變化，越來越多的人認識到必須把語言知識和文化知識結合起來才能順利地進行交際。只學習語言材料，不瞭解文化背景，猶如只抓住了外表而沒有領悟其精神。實際上，語言是文化的一部分，同時又是文化的載體，語言與文化密不可分。

全書分為人物篇、經濟篇、法律篇、教育篇、宗教篇、環保篇、文學篇和奧運篇八章。每章又分為文化背景知識補充、相關知識連結和練習三部分。以第一章人物篇為例，Mandela's Garden摘選自南非黑人領袖曼德拉的自傳，描述的是他在獄中的一段生活。在本書第一章第一節「文化背景知識補充」中你就能讀到中英文兩個版本的關於曼德拉的生平介紹。另外提到曼德拉，你可能還會想起另一位為消除種族歧視而做出不懈努力的黑人民權運動領袖馬丁· 路德· 金和美國歷史上首位非洲裔總統巴拉克· 歐巴馬，當然你也會在第二節「相關知識連結」中對他們進行瞭解。另外，在附錄二「演講名篇」中你還可以讀到馬丁· 路德· 金的演講名篇〈I Have a Dream〉及歐巴馬的就職演講。而這些對於英語學習者而言無疑是非常寶貴的學習和背誦材料。在每一章的第三節練習中還特別設計了相關的閱讀理解測試題，對書中出現的重點詞語、句型也進行了考察。從擴充詞彙量、鞏固語法、擴大閱讀量的角度上看，此書無疑會對英語學習者具有強烈的吸引力。

這本書從醞釀到完成歷時五年多，我們始終認為這是一件有意義的工作，在編寫過程中不斷徵求學生的意見，逐步探索。我們計劃在本書的基礎上繼續蒐集材料，擴充範圍，使該書的內容更加豐富，更有助於讀者學習英語。

編者

第一章 人物篇

第一節 文化背景知識補充

一、納爾遜· 曼德拉

【中文簡介】

納爾遜· 羅利赫拉赫拉· 曼德拉（Nelson Rolihlahla Mandela），1918年7月18日出生於南非特蘭斯凱的一個大酋長家庭，先後獲得南非大學文學士和威特沃特斯蘭德大學法學學士，當過律師。曼德拉自幼性格剛強，崇敬民族英雄，因為是家中長子而被指定為酋長繼承人。但他卻表示：「絕不願以酋長身分統治一個受壓迫的部族」，而要「以一個戰士的名義投身於民族解放事業」，毅然走上了追求民族解放的道路。1944年他加入了南非非洲國民大會（簡稱非國大）。1948年當選為非國大青年聯盟全國書記，1950年任非國大青年聯盟全國主席。1952年先後任非國大執委、德蘭士瓦省主席、全國副主席。同年年底，他成功地組織並領導了「蔑視不公正法令運動」，贏得了全體黑人的尊敬。為此，南非當局曾兩次發出不准他參加公眾集會的禁令。

1961年6 月曼德拉創建非國大軍事組織「民族之矛」，任總司令。1962 年8月，曼德拉被捕入獄，南非政府以政治煽動和非法越境罪判處他5年監禁，當時他年僅43歲。1964年6月，他又被指控犯有陰謀顛覆罪而改判為無期徒刑，從此開始了漫長的鐵窗生涯。他在獄中度過了長達27個春秋，備受迫害和折磨，但始終堅貞不屈。1990 年2 月11 日，南非當局在國內外輿論壓力下，被迫宣布無條件釋放曼德拉。同年3 月，他被非國大全國執委會任命為副主席、代行主席職務，並於1991 年7 月當選為主席。1994 年4 月，非國大在南非首次不分種族的大選中獲勝。同年5 月，曼德拉成為南非第一位黑人總統。1997 年12 月，曼德拉辭去非國大主席一職，並表示不再參加1999　年6　月的總統競選。1999年6月正式去職。

1991年聯合國教科文組織授予曼德拉「烏弗埃-博瓦尼爭取和平獎」。1993年10月，諾貝爾和平委員會授予他諾貝爾和平獎，以表彰他為廢除南非種族歧視政策所作出的貢獻。同年他還與當時的南非總統德克勒克一起被授予美國費城自由勛章。1998年9月曼德拉訪美，獲美國「國會金獎」，成為第一個獲得美國這一最高獎項的非洲人。2000年8月被南部非洲發展共同體授予「卡馬」勛章，以表彰他在領導南非人民爭取自由的長期鬥爭中，在實現新舊南非的和平過渡階段，以及擔任南共體主席期間作出的傑出貢獻。

1992年曼德拉與前妻溫妮分居，1996年3月19日，法院判定曼德拉與溫妮離婚。現任妻子格拉薩· 馬謝爾（Graca　Machel）是莫桑比克前總統薩莫拉的遺孀，1998年7月18日與曼德拉結婚。1992年10月曼德拉首次訪華，被北京大學授予名譽法學博士學位。1999年5月，曼德拉總統應邀訪華，成為首位訪華的南非國家元首。

曼德拉的主要著作有《走向自由之路不會平坦》、《鬥爭就是生活》、《爭取世界自由宣言》及自傳《漫漫自由路》。

【英文簡介】

Nelson Mandela (1918-2013) led the struggle to replace the apartheid regime of South Africa with a multi-racial democracy. He was imprisoned for 27 years and went on to become his country's first black president.

Rolihlahla Mandela was born in Transkei, South Africa on July 18th, 1918 and was given the name of Nelson by one of his teachers. His father Henry was a respected advisor to the Thembu royal family.

Mandela was educated at the University of Fort Hare and later at the University of Witwatersrand, qualifying in law in 1942. He became increasingly involved with

the African National Congress (ANC) , a multi-racial nationalist movement trying to bring about political change in South Africa.

In 1948, the National Party came to power and began to implement a policy of "apartheid", or forced segregation on the basis of race. The ANC staged a campaign of passive resistance against apartheid laws.In 1952, Mandela became one of the ANC's deputy presidents. By the late 1950s, faced with increasing government discrimination, Mandela, his friend Oliver Tambo, and some others began to move the ANC in a more radical direction. Mandela was tried for treason in 1956, but acquitted after a five-year trial.

In March 1960, sixty-nine black anti-apartheid demonstrators were killed by police at Sharpeville. The government declared a state of emergency and banned the ANC. In response, the organization abandoned its policy of non-violence and Mandela helped establish the ANC's military wing "Umkhonto we Sizwe" or "The Spear of the Nation". He was appointed its commander-in-chief and traveled abroad to receive military training and to find support for the ANC.

On his return he was arrested and sentenced to five years in prison. In 1963, Mandela and other ANC leaders were tried for plotting to overthrow the government by violence. The following year Mandela was sentenced to life imprisonment. He was held in Robben Island Prison, off the coast of Cape Town, and later in Pollsmoor Prison on the mainland. During his years in prison he became an international symbol of resistance to apartheid.

In 1990, the South African government responded to internal and international pressure and released Mandela, at the same time lifting the ban against the ANC. In 1991 Mandela became the ANC's leader.

He was awarded the Nobel Peace Prize together with F.W. de Klerk, then president of South Africa, in 1993. The following year South Africa held its first multiracial election and Mandela was elected its first black president. In 1998, he was married for the third time to Graça Machel, the widow of the president of Mozambique. Mandela's second wife, Winnie, whom he married in 1958 and divorced in 1996, remains a controversial anti-apartheid activist. In 1997 he stepped down as ANC leader and in 1999 his presidency of South Africa came to an end.

Mandela continues to support a variety of causes, particularly the fight against HIVAids. In 2004, Mandela announced he would be retiring from public life and his public appearances have become less and less frequent. On August 29, 2007, a permanent statue of Nelson Mandela was unveiled in Parliament Square, London.

Nelson Mandela is one of the great moral and political leaders of our time. Since his triumphant release in 1990 from more than a quarter-century of imprisonment, Mandela has been at the center of the most compelling and inspiring political drama in the world. Long Walk to Freedom: the Autobiography of Nelson Mandela was published in Boston, USA in 1994. It is a moving and exhilarating autobiography, a book destined to take its place among the finest memoirs of history's greatest figures.In this book, Nelson Rolihlahla Mandela tells the extraordinary story of his life-an epic of struggle, setback, renewed hope, and ultimate triumph.

To millions of people around the world, Nelson Mandela stands, as no other living figure does, for the triumph of dignity and hope over despair and hatred, of selfdiscipline and love over persecution and evil.

【詞彙】

apartheid	n.	（南非）種族隔離
regime	n.	政體，政權，政權制度
segregation	n.	種族隔離
controversial	adj.	爭論的，爭議的

statue n. 雕像

permanent adj. 永久的，持久的

triumphant adj. 勝利的，成功的，狂歡的，洋洋得意的

compelling adj. 強制的，強迫的，引人注目的

antiapartheid adj. 反種族隔離的

autobiography n. 自傳

persecution n. 迫害，煩擾

【問題】

1.What contribution did Nelson Mandela do to his country？

2.When and why Mandela was awarded the Nobel Peace Prize？

3.What is the meaning of apartheid？

二、史蒂芬·威廉·霍金

【中文簡介】

史蒂芬·威廉·霍金（Stephen William Hawking，1942—2018），1942年1月8日出生於英國牛津，曾先後畢業於牛津大學和劍橋大學，並獲劍橋大學哲學博士學位。他之所以在輪椅上坐了46年，是因為他在21歲時就不幸患上了肌肉萎縮性側索硬化症，演講和問答只能透過語音合成器來完成。但他卻成為英國劍橋大學應用數學及理論物理學系教授，當代最重要的廣義相對論和宇宙論家，是20世紀享有國際盛譽的偉人之一，被稱為在世的最偉大的科學家，還被稱為「宇宙之王」。

霍金出生的那一天剛好是伽利略逝世300週年紀念日。1970年代他與彭羅斯一起證明了著名的奇性定理，為此他們共同獲得了1988　年的沃爾夫物理獎。他也因此被譽為繼愛因斯坦之後世界上最著名的科學思想家和最傑出的理論物理學

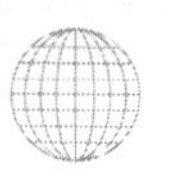

家。霍金還證明了黑洞的面積定理，即隨著時間的增加黑洞的面積不減。這很自然地使人將黑洞的面積和熱力學的熵聯繫在一起。1973年，在考慮黑洞附近的量子效應時，霍金發現黑洞會像黑體一樣發出輻射，其輻射的溫度和黑洞質量成反比，這樣黑洞就會因為輻射而慢慢變小，而溫度卻越變越高，並將以最後一刻的爆炸而告終。黑洞輻射的發現具有極其重要的意義，它將引力、量子力學和統計力學統一在了一起。

1974年以後，霍金的研究轉向了量子引力論。雖然現在還沒有得出一個確定的理論，但已經發現了一些特徵。例如，空間一時間在普郎克尺度（10—33公分）下不是平坦的，而是處於一種泡沫的狀態。在量子引力中不存在純態，因果性受到破壞，因此使不可知性從經典統計物理、量子統計物理提高到了量子引力的第三個層次。

1980年以後，霍金的興趣轉向了量子宇宙論。

2004年7月，霍金修正了自己原來的「黑洞悖論」觀點，認為訊息應該守恆。

2018年3月14日，霍金的家人發表聲明表示霍金去世，終年76歲。其骨灰的下葬儀式在2018年6月15日於倫敦西敏寺中殿的教堂中舉行。

霍金暢銷書——《時間簡史——從大爆炸到黑洞》

《時間簡史——從大爆炸到黑洞》（1988年撰寫）是霍金的代表作。作者想像豐富，構思奇妙，語言優美，字字珠璣，所描寫的世界之外，未來之變，是這樣的神奇和美妙。這本書至今累計發行量已達2500萬冊，已被譯成近40種語言。

本書的副標題是從大爆炸到黑洞。霍金認為他一生的貢獻是，在經典物理的框架裡，證明了黑洞和大爆炸奇點的不可避免性，黑洞會越變越大；但在量子物理的框架裡，他指出，黑洞因輻射而越變越小，大爆炸的奇點不但被量子效應所抹平，而且整個宇宙正是起始於此。

霍金

【英文簡介】

Stephen William Hawking （1942-2018）, British theoretical physicist and mathematician whose main field of research has been the beginning of the universe, and a unified theory of physics, the nature of space and time, including irregularities in space and time known as singularities （奇點）.

Hawking was born on 8 January, 1942 （300 years after the death of Galileo） in Oxford, England. In 1958 he entered Oxford University.

In 1961, he attended a summer course at the Royal Observatory.

In 1962, he completed his undergraduate courses and received a bachelor's degree in physics.

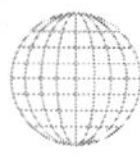

Then Hawking enrolled as a research student in general relativity at the department of applied mathematics and theoretical physics at the University of Cambridge.

In 1966, Hawking earned his Ph.D. Degree from Trinity College at the University of Cambridge.

In 1974, he became one of the youngest fellows of the Royal Society.

In 1977, he became a professor of physics after finishing his post-doctoral research at the University of Cambridge.

In 1979, he was appointed Lucasian Professor of Mathematics at Cambridge.

In the earliest stages, Hawking has been concerned with the concept of singularities breakdowns in space and time（奇性定理）. The most familiar example of a singularity is a black hole, the final form of a collapsed star.

During the late 1960s Hawking proved that a singularity must occur at the big bang（the explosion that marked the beginning of the universe and the birth of space-time itself）.

In 1970 Hawking turned to the examination of the properties of black holes: the surface area of the event horizon (the boundary of a black hole) around a black hole could only increase or remain constant with time; this area could never decrease.

Since 1974 Hawking has studied the behavior of matter in a black hole in quantum mechanics. Quantum mechanics （量子宇宙論） is a theory that describes black holes from which nothing was supposed to be able to escape could emit thermal radiation, or heat.

Throughout the 1990s Hawking sought to explain the universe by incorporating all four basic types of interactions between matter and energy: strong nuclear interactions, weak nuclear interactions, electromagnetic interactions, and gravitational interactions.

His Major Works:

Universe in a Nutshell（《果殼裡的宇宙》）

The Illustrated Brief History of Time （1988）（《時間簡史》（插圖本））

Black Holes and Baby Universes and Other Essays （1993） （《黑洞、嬰兒宇宙及其他》）

The Theory of Everything: The Origin and Fate of the Universe（《時空本性》

The Future of Space-time《未來的魅力》

A Brief History of Time: From the Big Bang to Black Holes《時間簡史——從大爆炸到黑洞》

In 1992 American filmmaker Errol Morris helped make the all-time best seller A Brief History of Time into a film about Hawking's life and work.

Words by Stephen Hawking:

I am quite often asked, "How do you feel about having ALS?"

The answer is, not a lot.I try to lead as normal a life as possible, and not think about my condition, or regret the things.

I have had motor neuron disease for practically all my adult life. I could select words from a series of menus on the screen, by pressing a switch in hands, head or eye movement.

A speech synthesizer fitted to my wheel chair allowed me to write, talk. Yet it has not prevented me from having a very attractive family, and success in my work.

It gave me something to live for. I realized that there were a lot of worthwhile things I could do.I was enjoying life in the present more than before.

Thanks to the help I have received from Jane, my children, and a large number of other people. I have been lucky, that my condition has progressed more slowly than is often the case. But it shows that one need not lose hope.

【問題】

1.What is ALS?

2.What is Hawking's main field of research?

3.Which sentence by Hawking moves you the most?

第二節 相關知識連結

一、馬丁· 路德· 金

【中文簡介】

馬丁· 路德· 金（1929年1月15日—1968年4月4日），著名的美國民權運動領袖，誕生於美國東南部的喬治亞州的亞特蘭大市。1948 年他大學畢業，擔任教會的牧師。1948年到1951年間，馬丁· 路德· 金在美國東海岸的費城繼續深造。1963年，馬丁· 路德· 金晉見了甘迺迪總統，要求通過新的民權法，給黑人以平等的權利。同年8月28日在林肯紀念堂前發表《我有一個夢想》的演說。他在1964年獲得諾貝爾和平獎，有金牧師之稱。1968 年4 月，馬丁· 路德· 金前往孟菲斯市領導工人罷工，下榻洛林汽車旅館。4日晚飯前，他站在二樓300號房間的陽臺上，與人談話。這時在街對面的一幢公寓裡，一個狙擊手端著一架帶有觀測鏡的步槍，向他射去。子彈從前面穿過他的脖子，他隨即倒地。

馬丁· 路德· 金

【英文簡介】

Martin Luther King, Jr. (January 15, 1929 -April 4, 1968) was an American clergyman, activist and prominent leader in the African-American Civil Rights Movement. His main legacy was to secure progress on civil rights in the United States and he is frequently referenced as a human rights icon today.

A Baptist minister, King became a civil rights activist early in his career. He led the 1955 Montgomery Bus Boycott and helped found the Southern Christian Leadership Conference in 1957, serving as its first president.

King's efforts led to the 1963 March on Washington, where King delivered his "I Have a Dream" speech. There, he raised public consciousness of the civil rights movement and established himself as one of the greatest orators in the U.S. history.

In 1964, King became the youngest person to receive the Nobel Peace Prize for his work to end racial segregation and racial discrimination through civil disobedience and other non-violent means. By the time of his death in 1968, he had refocused his efforts on ending poverty and opposing the Vietnam War, both from a religious perspective.

King was assassinated on April 4, 1968 in Memphis, Tennessee. He was posthumously awarded the Presidential Medal of Freedom in 1977 and the Congressional Gold Medal in 2004. And Martin Luther King, Jr.Day was established as a U.S. national holiday in 1986.

【詞彙】

clergyman n. 牧師，教士

legacy n. 遺贈（物），遺產（祖先傳下來）

icon n. 圖標，肖像，偶像

consciousness n. 意識，知覺，自覺，覺悟，個人思想

orator n. 演説者，演講者，雄辯家，〔律〕原告，請願人

discrimination n. 辨別，區別，識別力，辨別力，歧視

assassinate vt. 暗殺，行刺

emancipation n. 釋放，解放

【問題】

1.Why Martin Luther King, Jr.is frequently referenced as a human rights icon today?

2.When and where King was assassinated?

二、巴拉克· 歐巴馬

巴拉克· 歐巴馬

【中文簡介】

巴拉克· 歐巴馬，1961年出生，民主黨人，一個充滿傳奇的「美國夢」代言人。因為繼父是印度尼西亞人，他曾叫巴利· 索托洛。他還在「亞洲叢林」中接受過四年的東方教育，對印度尼西亞有著田園詩般的美好回憶。由於他的肯亞祖先信奉伊斯蘭教，而他本人在印度尼西亞的穆斯林上過學，直到大選，人們還有意無意地稱他為巴拉克· 侯賽因· 歐巴馬。一些美國人選他為總統，理由是這樣一來中東的恐怖分子就失去了襲擊美國的理由。

歐巴馬2000年競選國會眾議員時遭到失敗，但是八年後，他竟然突破重圍，先是擊敗前「第一夫人」希拉蕊獲得民主黨提名，然後又以較大優勢擊敗獲得過多枚勛章的「越戰英雄」、共和黨人麥肯，一躍成為美國歷史上第一位黑人總統和少數年輕總統之一。

幸運與傳奇並不能畫等號。歐巴馬的經歷是一個艱難創業、克服困難、不斷進取、自我反省和塑造的旅程。他初到印度尼西亞時語言不通，但僅用了四年就融入了印度尼西亞社會，而時隔四十年後仍然能說一口流利的印度尼西亞語；他受到過種族歧視，並一度為身分煩惱而想要「自我毀滅」，但是，他迅速從書本和運動中找到了答案；他志願到社區和教堂從事低薪職業，因為他堅信自我救贖依賴於集體救贖，他要為底層民眾服務；他是《哈佛法律評論》歷史上的第一位黑人主編，但是他放棄了高薪聘請和優厚條件，選擇到一家低收入的民權律師事務所工作，為民眾申冤。

在參加政治競選和任伊利諾伊州參議員與國會參議員期間，他看到了活生生的「抹黑政治」及其對國家的危害，認識到了美國信仰、價值觀和政黨的分裂。因此，他牢記林肯「分裂之家不能長久」的格言，立志要透過努力消除這種弊端。不管他是否能夠改變這種局面，他的「改變」口號都給了處於經濟危機的美國人以極大的振奮。

「改變」的口號，遠離華盛頓政客的行為方式，對競爭對手的寬容精神以及體恤民生的生活經歷，是他贏得美國人民喜愛的最根本原因。而這就是「美國夢」得以實現的根基。從競選國會議員失敗到當選總統，他僅用了八年時間，被視為現代版的「美國夢」代言人，甘迺迪的衣鉢傳人。

2008年11月4日，47歲的巴拉克·歐巴馬以非洲裔的身分當選為美國第44任總統，打破了白人壟斷美國總統的歷史。

【英文簡介】

When Barack Obama was welcomed as the first black president in America, we all know a great change has come too.

Barack Hussein Obama was born on August 4, 1961, in Honolulu, Hawaii. Obama's parents separated when he was two years old and later divorced. Obama's father went to Harvard to pursue his Ph.D. degree and then returned to Kenya.

He was enrolled in the fifth grade at the esteemed Punahou Academy, graduating with honors in 1979. He was only one of the three black students at the school. This is where Obama first became conscious of racism and what it meant to be an African-American.

After high school, Obama studied at Occidental College in Los Angeles for two years. He then transferred to Columbia University in New York, graduating in 1983 with a degree in political science.

Obama entered Harvard Law School in 1988. In February 1990, he was elected the first African-American editor of the Harvard Law Review. Obama graduated magna cum laude in 1991.

After law school, Obama returned to Chicago to practice as a civil rights lawyer, joining the firm of Miner, Barnhill & Galland.He also taught at the University of Chicago Law School. And he helped organize voter registration drives during Bill Clinton's 1992 presidential campaign.

Obama published an autobiography in 1995 Dreams from My Father: a Story of Race and Inheritance. And he won a Grammy for the audio version of the book.

Obama's advocacy work led him to run for the Illinois State Senate as a Democrat. He was elected in 1996 from the south side neighborhood of Hyde Park.

During these years, Obama worked with both Democrats and Republicans in drafting legislation on ethics, expanded health care services and early childhood education programs for the poor. He also created a state earned-income tax credit for the working poor.

In the November 2004 general election, Obama received 70% of the vote to Keyes's 27%, the largest electoral victory in Illinois history. Obama became the third African-American elected to the U.S.Senate since Reconstruction.

His second book, The Audacity of Hope: Thoughts on Reclaiming the American Dream, was published in October 2006.

In February 2007, Obama made headlines when he announced his candidacy for the 2008 Democratic presidential nomination. He was locked in a tight battle with former first lady and current U.S. Senator from New York, Hillary Rodham Clinton until he became the presumptive nominee on June 3, 2008. On November 4, 2008, Obama defeated Republican presidential nominee John McCain for the position of U.S. President. He is now the 44th president of the United States.

【問題】

1.When and where did Obama first become conscious of racism and what it meant to be an African-American?

2.What's the meaning of the phrase "be locked in a tight battle" ?

3.Is Obama the 44th or the 45th president of the United States?

第三節 練習

1.Match the synonymic phrases.

A.at heart a.to be responsible for

B.at great length b.to be thinking with pleasure about sth that is going to happen

C.to read into c.at the bottom of one's heart, in essence

D.to bring back to health/life d.to continue

E.to be in charge e.to supply with; to offer

F.to look forward to f.to assume that sth means more than it does

G.to get in touch with g.to be in prison

H.to be behind bars h.makes sb/sth healthy again

I.to go on i.to contact sb

J.to provide with　　　　　　　　　　j.for a long time

2.Translate the following sentences into English.

（1）要在監獄中生存下來，一個人得找到一些對自己日常生活感到滿意的方式。

（2）當權者不會為給了我許可而後悔，因為菜地一開始繁盛，我就常常給典獄長們送去一些最好的番茄和大蔥。

（3）播撒下種子，看著它成長，照顧它然後獲得豐收，這給了我一種簡單但綿延不絕的滿足感。

（4）儘管我一直很喜歡園藝，但是直到入獄後我才終於可以照料我自己的菜地。

（5）我沒有書中提到的很多材料，但是我透過嘗試和失敗進行學習。

3.Paraphrase. Tell the meanings of the following sentences in your own words.

（1） The free time also allowed me to pursue what became two of my favorite hobbies on Robben Island.

（2） The sense of being the owner of the small patch of earth offered a small taste of freedom.

（3） The end of manual labor was liberating.

（4） I do not know what she read into that letter.

（5） The early harvests were poor, but they soon improved.

4.Cloze. Fill in the blanks according to the text: Mandela's Garden.

While I have always （1）gardening, it was not until I was behind （2） that I was able to （3）my own garden. My first experience in the garden was at Fort Hare, as part of university's （4）labor requirement, I worked in one of my （5）garden and enjoyed the （6）with the soil as an （7）to my intellectual labors. Once I was in Johannesburg studying and then working, I had neither the time nor the space to start a garden.

I began to （8）books on gardening.I studied different gardening （9） and types of fertilizers. I did not have many of the （10）that the books discussed, but I learned through trial and （11）.For a time, I （12）to grow peanuts, and used different soils and fertilizers, but finally I gave up. It was one of my few （13）.

A garden was one of the few things in prison that one could （14）. To plant a seed, watch it grow, to tend it and （15）it, offered a simple but （16） satisfaction. The （17）of being the （18）of the small patch of earth （19）a small taste of （20）.

5.Complete each of the following sentences with the most likely answer.

（1） My daughter has walked eight miles today. We never guessed that she could walk ______far.

A./ B.such C.that D.as

（2） The statistics ______that living standards in the area have improved drastically in recent times.

A.proves B.is proving C.are proving D.prove

（3） There are only ten apples left in the baskets, ______the spoilt ones.

A.not counting B.not to count

C.don't count D.having not counted

（4） It was______we had hoped

A.more a success than B.a success more than

C.as much of a success as D.a success as much as

（5） There used to be a petrol station near the park, ______?

A.didn't it B.doesn't there C.usedn't it D.didn't there

(6) It is an offence to show______against people of different races.

A.distinction B.difference C.separation D.discrimination

(7) A great amount of work has gone into______the Cathedral to its previous splendor.

A.refreshing B.restoring C.renovating D.renewing

(8) The thieves fled with the local police close on their______.

A.backs B.necks C.toes D.heels

(9) The economic recession has meant that job______is a rare thing.

A.security B.safety C.protection D.secureness

(10) Many people nowadays save money to______for their old age.

A.cater B.supply C.provide D.equip

6.Reading comprehension.

When Franklin D. Roosevelt was elected President of the United States in 1932, not only the United States but also the rest of the world was in the throes of an economic depression. Following the termination of World War I, Britain and the United States at first experienced a boom in industry. Called the Roaring Twenties, the 1920s ushered in a number of things—prosperity, greater equality for women in the work world, rising consumption, and easy credit. The outlook for American business was rosy.

October 1929 was a month that had catastrophic economic reverberations worldwide. The American stock market witnessed the "Great Crash", as it is called, and the temporary boom in the American economy came to a standstill. Stock prices sank, and panic spread. The ensuing unemployment soared to 12 million by 1932.

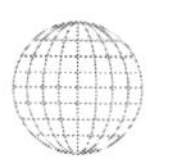

Germany in the postwar years suffered from burdensome compensation it was obliged to pay to the Allies. The country's industrial capacity had been greatly diminished by the war.Inflation, political instability, and high unemployment were factors helpful to the growth of the initial Nazi party. Germans had lost confidence in their old leaders and heralded the arrival of a messiah-like figure who would lead them out of their economic wilderness. Hitler promised jobs and, once elected, kept his promise by providing employment in the party, in the newly expanded army, and in munitions factories.

Roosevelt was elected because he promised a "New Deal" to lift the United States out of the doldrums of the depression. Following the principles advocated by Keynes, a British economist, Roosevelt collected the spending capacities of the federal government to provide welfare, work, and agricultural aid to the millions of down-and-out Americans. Elected President for four terms because of his innovative policies, Roosevelt succeeded in dragging the nation out of the depression before the outbreak of World War Ⅱ.

（1） Which of the following was NOT true at the time Roosevelt was elected?

A.Stock prices were recovering slowly.

B.The nation was in a deep depression.

C.There were 12 million unemployed workers.

D.The nation needed help from the federal government.

（2） The "Great Crash" in the passage refers to ______.

A.the end of World War Ⅰ

B.the Great Depression

C.high unemployment rate

D.a slump in the stock market

（3） We can infer that the author of this passage ______.

A.disapproves of Roosevelt's "New Deal"

B.thinks the Depression could have been avoided

C.blames the Depression on the "Great Crash"

D.feels there was some similarity between Roosevelt and Hitler

（4） The best title for the passage is ______.

A.The Twenties

B.The Great Crash

C.The Depression

D.The End of World War I

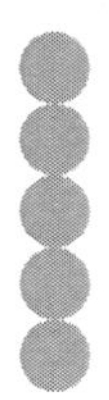

第二章 經濟篇

第一節 文化背景知識補充

一、亞洲金融危機

【中文簡介】

1997年7月2日，亞洲金融風暴席捲泰國，泰銖貶值。不久，這場風暴橫掃了馬來西亞、新加坡、日本和韓國等地，打破了亞洲經濟飛速發展的景象。亞洲一些經濟大國的經濟開始衰退，一些國家的政局也開始混亂。

亞洲金融危機爆發的原因有以下幾個方面：

1.亞洲國家的經濟形態

新、馬、泰、日、韓等國都為外向型經濟的國家。它們對世界市場的依賴性很大。亞洲經濟的動搖難免會出現牽一髮而動全身的狀況。以泰國為例，泰銖在國際市場上的買賣不由政府來主宰，而泰國本身並沒有足夠的外匯儲備，面對金融家的炒作，泰國經濟便不堪一擊。而經濟決定政治，所以，泰國政局也就動盪了。

2.美國的經濟利益和政策

1949年，共產中國的成立代表著社會主義陣營的建立。美國作為資本主義頭號強國，有了危機感，於是便透過強大的經濟後盾在亞太地區建立起一個資本主義的統一戰線：韓國、日本直至東南亞，都成了美國的經濟附庸。這給亞洲一些國家的飛速發展帶來了經濟支持。1970年代，東南亞一些國家的經濟迅猛發展就得益於此。但是，1991年，蘇聯解體代表著社會主義陣營的瓦解。美國當然不允許亞洲經濟繼續如此發展，於是就開始收回它的經濟損失。對於索羅斯的行為，美國採取縱容的態度。

3.喬治· 索羅斯及支持他的資本主義集團

「金融大鱷」、「一隻假寐的老狼」是對喬治· 索羅斯這個金融怪才的稱謂。他曾說過，「在金融運作方面，說不上有道德還是無道德，這只是一種操作。金融市場是不屬於道德範疇的，它不是不道德的，這裡根本不存在道德，因為它有自己的遊戲規則。我是金融市場的參與者，我會按照已定的規則來玩這個遊戲，我不會違反這些規則，所以我不覺得內疚或要負責任。從亞洲金融風暴這個事情來講，我是否炒作對金融事件的發生不會起任何作用。我不炒作它照樣會發生。我並不覺得炒外幣、投機有什麼不道德。另一方面我遵守運作規則。我尊重那些規則，關心這些規則。作為一個有道德和關心它們的人，我希望確保這些規則，是有利於建立一個良好的社會的，所以我主張改變某些規則。我認為一些規則需要改進。如果改進和改良影響到我自己的利益，我還是會支持它，因為需要改良的這個規則也許正是事件發生的原因。」眾所周知，索羅斯對泰銖的炒作是亞洲金融風暴的導火線。他是一個絕對有實力，有能力的金融家，然而透過玩弄亞洲國家政權，來達到自己獲得巨額資本的目的顯然是卑劣的。

【英文簡介】

The Asian Financial Crisis was a period of financial crisis that gripped much of Asia beginning in July 1997, and raised fears of a worldwide economic meltdown due to financial contagion.

The crisis started in Thailand with the financial collapse of the Thai baht caused by the decision of the Thai government to float the baht, cutting its peg to the USD, after exhaustive efforts to support it in the face of a severe financial overextension that was in part real estate driven.At the time, Thailand had acquired a burden of foreign debt that made the country effectively bankrupt even before the collapse of its currency. As the crisis spread, most of Southeast Asia and Japan saw slumping currencies, devalued stock markets and other asset prices, and a precipitous rise in private debt.

Though there has been general agreement on the existence of a crisis and its consequences, what is less clear is the causes of the crisis, as well as its scope and resolution. Indonesia, South Korea and Thailand were the countries most affected by the crisis.Hong Kong of PRC, Malaysia, Laos and the Philippines were also hurt by the slump. The People's Republic of China, India, Taiwan of China, Singapore, Brunei and Vietnam were less affected, although all suffered from a loss of demand and confidence throughout the region.

Foreign debt-to-GDP ratios rose from 100% to 167% in the four large ASEAN economies in 1993-1996, and then shot up beyond 180% during the worst of the crisis. In South Korea, the ratios rose from 13% to 21% and then as high as 40%, while the other Northern NICs (Newly Industrialized Countries) fared much better. Only in Thailand and South Korea did debt service-to-exports ratios rise.

Although most of the governments of Asia had seemingly sound fiscal policies, the International Monetary Fund (IMF) stepped in to initiate a ＄40 billion program to stabilize the currencies of South Korea, Thailand, and Indonesia, economies particularly hard hit by the crisis. The efforts to stem a global economic crisis did little to stabilize the domestic situation in Indonesia, however. After 30 years in power, President Suharto was forced to step down in May 1998 in the wave of widespread rioting that followed sharp price increases caused by a drastic devaluation of the rupiah. The effects of the crisis lingered through 1998. In the Philippines growth dropped to virtually zero in 1998. Only Singapore and Taiwan of China proved relatively insulated from the shock, but both suffered serious hits in passing, the former more so due to its size and geographical location between Malaysia and Indonesia. By 1999, however, analysts saw signs that the economies of Asia were beginning to recover.

【詞彙】

baht	n.	泰國銖，貨幣單位
contagion	n.	傳染，蔓延
devalue	v.	貶值
fiscal	adj.	財政的
grip	v.	緊握，抓緊
insulate	v.	使隔離
meltdown	n.	徹底垮臺
peg	n.	釘，栓
ratio	n.	比，比率
riot	n.	騷亂
slump	n.	衰退，物價暴跌

【問題】

1.What is Asian Financial Crisis?

2.Where did the crisis begin?

3.How much money did IMF initiate to stabilize the Asian Financial Crisis?

二、大蕭條

【中文簡介】

大蕭條，是指1929年至1933年的全球性經濟大衰退。大蕭條的影響比歷史上任何一次經濟衰退都更為深遠。這次經濟衰退以農產品價格下跌為起點：首先是木材價格下跌（1928年），這主要是由蘇聯的木材競爭造成的；隨後更大的災難於1929年到來了，加拿大小麥生產過量，美國強迫壓低所有農產品產地基本穀物的價格。不管是歐洲、美洲還是澳大利亞，農業衰退都因為金融的大崩潰而進一步惡化。尤其在美國，一股投機熱導致大量資金從歐洲抽回，隨後在1929年10月發生了令人恐慌的華爾街股市暴跌。1931年法國銀行家收回了給奧地利銀行的貸款，但還是不足以償還債務。這場災難使中歐和東歐許多國家的制度破產：德國銀行家為了自保而延期償還外債，進而危及在德國有很大投資的英國銀行家。資本的短缺，在所有的工業化國家中，都帶來了出口和國內消費的銳減：沒有市場必然導致工廠關閉，貨物越少，貨物運輸也就越少，這必然會危害船運業和造船業。在所有國家中，經濟衰退的後果都是大規模失業：美國1370萬，德國560萬，英國280萬（1932年的最大數據）。大蕭條對拉丁美洲也有重大影響，使得在這個幾乎被歐美銀行家和商人企業家完全支配的地區失去了外資和商品出口。

大蕭條

大蕭條的普遍影響導致了：

1.提高了政府對經濟的政策參與性，即凱恩斯主義；

2.以關稅的形式強化了經濟的民族主義；

3.激起了作為共產主義替代物的浪漫——極權主義政治運動（如德國納粹）。大蕭條相對於其他單一原因來說是最能夠解釋為什麼在1932年到1938年期間歐洲大陸和拉丁美洲各國政治逐漸右翼化；

4.阿道夫· 希特勒、貝尼托· 墨索里尼等獨裁者的崛起，間接導致了第二次世界大戰的爆發。

【英文簡介】

The Great Depression was a worldwide economic downturn starting in most places in 1929 and ending at different times in the 1930s or early 1940s for different countries. It was the largest and most important economic depression in the 20th century, and is used in the 21st century as an example of how far the world's economy can fall. The Great Depression originated in the United States; historians most often use as a starting date the day of the stock market crash on October 29, 1929, known as Black Tuesday.

The depression had devastating effects in virtually every country, rich or poor.International trade plunged by half to two-thirds, as did personal income, tax revenue, prices and profits. Cities all around the world were hit hard, especially those dependent on heavy industry. Construction was virtually halted in many countries. Farming and rural areas suffered as crop prices fell by roughly 60 percent. Facing plummeting demand with few alternate sources of jobs, areas dependent on primary sector industries such as farming, mining and logging suffered the most. However, even shortly after the Wall Street Crash of 1929, optimism persisted; John D.Rockefeller said that "here are days when many are discouraged. In the 93 years of my life, depressions have come and gone. Prosperity has always returned and will again."

The Great Depression ended at different times in different countries. In America it ended in 1941 with America's entry into World War II. The majority of countries set up relief programs, and most underwent some sort of political upheaval, which pushed them to the left or right.In some states, the desperate citizens turned toward nationalist demagogues—the most infamous being Adolf Hitler—setting the stage for World War II in 1939.

The Great Depression was triggered by a sudden, total collapse in the stock market. The stock market turned upward in early 1930, returning to early 1929 levels by April, though still almost 30 percent below the peak of September 1929. Government and business actually spent more in the first half of 1930 than in the corresponding period of the previous year. But consumers, many of whom had suffered severe losses in the stock market the previous year, cut back their expenditures by ten percent, and a severe drought ravaged the agricultural heartland of the USA beginning in the summer of 1930.

In early 1930, credit was ample and available at low rates, but people were reluctant to add new debt. By May 1930, auto sales had declined to below the levels of 1928. Prices in general began to decline, but wages held steady in 1930, then began to drop in 1931. Conditions were worse in farming areas, where commodity prices plunged, and in mining and logging areas, where unemployment was high and there were few other jobs. The decline in the US economy was the factor that pulled down most other countries at first, and then internal weaknesses or strengths in each country made conditions worse or better.Frantic attempts to shore up the economies of individual nations through protectionist policies, such as the 1930 U.S. Smoot-Hawley Tariff Act and retaliatory tariffs in other countries, exacerbated the collapse in global trade. By late in 1930, a steady decline set in and reached bottom by March 1933.

Political Consequences

The crisis had many political consequences, among which was the abandonment of classic economic liberal approaches, which Roosevelt replaced in the United States with Keynesian policies. These policies magnified the role of the federal government in the national economy. Between 1933 and 1939, federal expenditure tripled, and Roosevelt's critics charged that he was turning America into a socialist state. The Great Depression was a main factor in the implementation of social democracy and planned economies in European countries after World War Ⅱ. (See Marshall Plan). Although Austrian economists had challenged Keynesianism since the 1920s, it was not until the 1970s, with the influence of Milton Friedman that the Keynesian approach was politically questioned.

【詞彙】

alternate	adj.	交替的，輪換的
ample	adj.	充足的，豐富的
devastate	v.	破壞
halt	n.	停止
Keynesian	n.	凱恩斯主義
logging	n.	伐木搬運業
plunge	v.	跳進，投入
retaliatory	adj.	報復的
tariff	n.	關稅
virtually	adv.	事實上，實質上

【問題】

1.What is the Great Depression?

2.What are the economic effects of the Great Depression?

3.What are the political consequences of the Great Depression?

第二節 相關知識連結

次貸危機

【中文簡介】

次貸危機（subprime crisis），又稱次級房貸危機，也譯為次債危機，是指發生在美國的一場因次級抵押貸款機構破產、投資基金被迫關閉、股市劇烈震盪引起的金融風暴。它致使全球主要金融市場出現流動性不足的危機。美國「次貸危機」是從2006年春季開始逐步顯現的。2007年8月開始席捲美國、歐盟和日本等世界主要金融市場。次貸危機目前已經成為國際上的一個焦點問題。

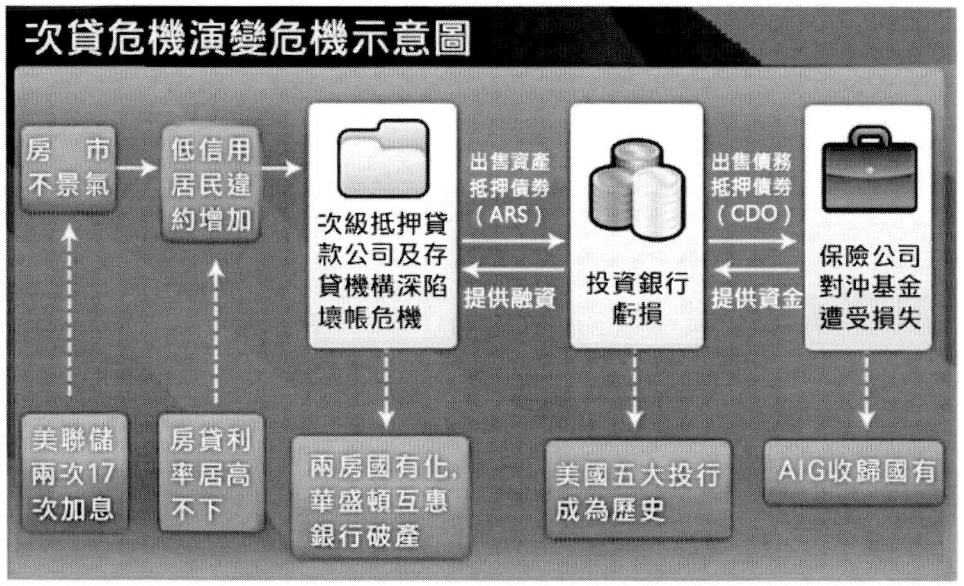

次貸危機定義

次貸即「次級貸款貸款」（subprime mortgage loan），「次」是與「高」、「優」相對應的，形容較差的一方，在「次貸危機」一詞中指的是信用低，還債能力差。

次級抵押貸款是一個高風險、高收益的行業，指一些貸款機構向信用程度較低和收入不高的借款人提供的貸款。與傳統意義上的標準抵押貸款的區別在於，次級抵押貸款對貸款者信用記錄和還款能力要求不高，貸款利率相應地比一般抵押貸款要高很多。那些因信用記錄不好或償還能力較弱而被銀行拒絕提供優質抵押貸款的人，會申請次級抵押貸款購買住房。

在房價不斷走高時，次級抵押貸款生意興隆。即使貸款人現金流並不足以償還貸款，他們也可以透過房產增值獲得再貸款來填補缺口。但當房價持平或下跌時，就會出現資金缺口而形成壞帳。

【英文簡介】

The subprime mortgage crisis is an ongoing financial crisis triggered by a dramatic rise in mortgage delinquencies and foreclosures in the United States, with major adverse consequences for banks and financial markets around the globe. The crisis, which has its roots in the closing years of the 20th century, became apparent in 2007 and has exposed pervasive weaknesses in financial industry regulation and the global financial system.

Approximately 80% of U.S.mortgages issued in recent years to subprime borrowers were adjustable-rate mortgage. When U.S.house prices began to decline in 2006-2007, refinancing became more difficult and as adjustable-rate mortgages began to reset at higher rates, mortgage delinquencies soared. Securities backed with subprime mortgages, widely held by financial firms, lost most of their value. The result has been a large decline in the capital of many banks and U.S. government sponsored enterprises, tightening credit around the world.

The immediate cause or trigger of the crisis was the bursting of the United States housing bubble which peaked in approximately 2005 -2006. High default rates on「subprime」and adjustable rate mortgages (ARM) began to increase quickly thereafter. An increase in loan incentives such as easy initial terms and a long-term

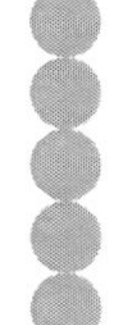

trend of rising housing prices had encouraged borrowers to assume difficult mortgages in the belief they would be able to quickly refinance at more favorable terms. However, once interest rates began to rise and housing prices started to drop moderately in 2006-2007 in many parts of the U.S., refinancing became more difficult. Defaults and foreclosure activity increased dramatically as easy initial terms expired, home prices failed to go up as anticipated, and ARM interest rates reset higher. Foreclosures accelerated in the United States in late 2006 and triggered a global financial crisis through 2007 and 2008.

In the years leading up to the crisis, high consumption and low savings rates in the U.S. contributed to significant amounts of foreign money flowing into the U.S.from fast-growing economies in Asia and oil-producing countries. This inflow of funds combined with low U.S. interest rates from 2002 - 2004 resulted in easy credit conditions, which fueled both housing and credit bubbles.Loans of various types (e.g., mortgage, credit card, and auto) were easy to obtain and consumers assumed an unprecedented debt load. As part of the housing and credit booms, the amount of financial agreements called mortgage-backed securities (MBS), which derive their value from mortgage payments and housing prices, greatly increased.Such financial innovation enabled institutions and investors around the world to invest in the U.S. housing market. As housing prices declined, major global financial institutions that had borrowed and invested heavily in subprime MBS reported significant losses. Defaults and losses on other loan types also increased significantly as the crisis expanded from the housing market to other parts of the economy. Total losses are estimated in the trillions of U.S. dollars globally.

While the housing and credit bubbles built, a series of factors caused the financial system to become increasingly fragile. Policymakers did not recognize the increasingly important role played by financial institutions such as investment banks and hedge funds, also known as the shadow banking system. Some experts believe these institutions had become as important as commercial (depository) banks in providing credit to the U.S. economy, but they were not subject to the same regulations. Institutions as well as certain regulated banks had also assumed significant debt burdens while providing the loans described above and did not have a financial cushion sufficient to absorb large loan defaults or MBS losses. These losses impacted the ability of financial institutions to lend, slowing economic activity. Concerns regarding the stability of key financial institutions drove central banks to take action to provide funds to encourage lending and to restore faith in the commercial paper markets, which are integral to funding business operations.Governments also bailed out key financial institutions, assuming significant additional financial commitments.

The risks to the broader economy created by the housing market downturn and subsequent financial market crisis were primary factors in several decisions by central banks around the world to cut interest rates and governments to implement economic stimulus packages. Effects on global stock markets due to the crisis have been dramatic.Between January 1 and October 11, 2008, owners of stocks in the U.S. corporations had suffered about＄8 trillion in losses, as their holdings declined in value from＄20 trillion to ＄12 trillion. Losses in other countries have averaged about 40% . Losses in the stock markets and housing value declines place further downward pressure on consumer spending, a key economic engine.Leaders of the larger developed and emerging nations met in November 2008 and March 2009 to formulate strategies for addressing the crisis.As of April 2009, many of the root causes of the crisis had yet to be addressed. A variety of solutions have been proposed by government officials, central bankers, economists, and business executives.

【詞彙】

adverse	adj.	不利的，相反的
default	n.	違約，拖欠債務

delinquency	n.	違約行為，過失
downturn	n.	下降，衰退
formulate	v.	制定，形成
foreclosure	n.	喪失抵押品贖回權
implement	v.	執行
incentive	adj.	激勵的
mortgage	n.	房屋抵押貸款
stimulus	n.	刺激
trigger	v.	引發，引起，觸發
unprecedented	adj.	空前的，史無前例的

【問題】

1.What is subprime mortgage crisis?

2.What is the immediate cause of the crisis?

3.How much losses have the stock owners of American corporations suffered in 2008?

第三節 練 習

1.Translate the phrases.

A.雙刃劍	B.國家主權	C.貿易協商
D.經濟實體	E.不恰當的政策	F.不平衡的貿易
G.經濟合作與發展組織	H.繁榮一衰退週期	I.隨之而來的金融危機

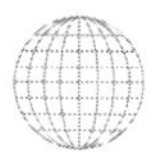

2.Translate the following sentences into English.

（1）在新世紀即將到來之際，全球化是一把雙刃劍。

（2）從某些方面來說，全球化僅僅是一個古老進程的時髦字眼。

（3）從1940年代末期至1980年代的「冷戰」致使美國捍衛貿易自由化和經濟發展，以此作為對抗共產主義的一種方式。

（4）在兩次世界大戰之後，歐洲各國視經濟一體化為治療致命的民族主義的一劑良藥。

（5）全球化繼續著它的進程，但至少在一個關鍵方面也背離著它。

3.Paraphrase. Tell the meanings of the following sentences in your own words.

（1） A decade later, even after Asia's 1997-1998 financial crisis, private capital flows dwarf governmental flows.

（2） The recent takeover struggle between British and German wireless giants is exceptional only for its size and bitterness.

（3） Meanwhile, Latin America and sub-Saharan Africa—whose embrace of the world economy has been late or limited—fared much less.

（4） The Asian financial crisis raised questions on both counts.

（5） What prevented the Asian crisis from becoming a full-scale economic downturn has been the astonishing U.S. economy.

4.Cloze. Fill in the blanks according to the text：Globalization's Dual Power.

Just because globalization is largely （1）propelled by better （2）and transportation—does not mean that it is （3）or completely （4）. Governments can, in subtle and not-so-subtle ways, （5）local industries and workers against （6）or （7）against foreign （8）. If only a few countries do, their actions will not （9）much. Global （10）and trade will go where they are most welcome and （11）. Indeed, it is （12）this logic that has （13）so many countries to accept

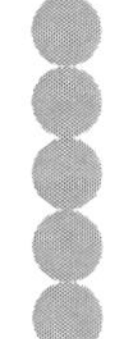

globalization. (14) by their behavior, most governments believe they have more to gain than to lose.

But this does not mean that a powerful popular (15), with (16) consequences, is not possible.In a global (17), too many sellers will be (18) too few buyers. A (19) presumption is that practical politicians would try to protect their (20) from global guts.

5.Complete each of the following sentences with the most likely answer.

(1) He's 26. It's high time he______a trade to make a living.

A.Learn B.learns C.must learn D.learned

(2) ______with confidence, Dr.Wang skillfully performed the operation.

A.To be filled B.Having been filled

C.Being filled D.Filled

(3) ______the harmful effects of smoking, he decided to give it up.

A.Convinced of B.Convincing

C.Convincing of D.Convinced by

(4) Making mistakes can teach you______you could do differently

A.what B.how C.when D.why

(5) The students strongly objected to______as teenagers.

A.be treated B.treating C.being treated D.treat

(6) Busy______he is, he always finds time for sports.

A.as B.though C.since D.if

(7) A woman has to be______a man to go half as far.

A.as twice good as B.twice better as

C.twice so good as D.twice as good as

（8） There is no denying the fact______quite many insects are dying out.

A.that B.why C.how D.which

（9） The first thing you should have learned at college is to work on your own. It's time you______able to manage your time.

A.could be B.should be C.were D.are

（10） On TV every taxi driver looks as if he had nothing______to drive 90 miles an hour trying to keep up with another car, often in pouring rain.

A.more to do but B.better to do than

C.else to do except D.interesting to do besides

6.Reading comprehension.

The three biggest lies in America are: （1） "The check is in the mail." （2） "Of course I'll respect you in the morning." （3） "It was a computer error."

Of these three little white lies, the worst of the lot by far is the third. It's the only one that can never be true. Today, if a bank statement cheats you out of 900 that way, you know what the clerk is sure to say: "It was a computer error." Nonsense, the computer is reporting nothing more than what the clerk typed into it. The most irritating case of all is when the computerized cash register in the grocery store shows that an item costs more than it actually does. If the innocent buyer points out the mistake, the checker, bagger, and manager all come together and offer the familiar explanation: "It was a computer error."

It wasn't, of course. That high-tech cash register is really nothing more than an electric eye. The eye reads the Universal Product Code—that ribbon of black and white lines in a corner of the package—and then checks the code against a price list stored in memory. If the price list is right, you'll be charged accurately.

Grocery stores update the price list each day—that is, somebody sits at a keyboard and types in the prices.If the price they type in is too high, there are only two explanations: carelessness or dishonesty. But somehow "a computer error" is supposed to excuse everything.

One reason we let people hide behind a computer is the common misperception that huge, modern computers are "electric brains" with "artificial intelligence." At some point there might be a machine with intelligence, but none exists today. The smartest computer on earth right now is no more "intelligent" than your average screwdriver. At this point in the development of computers, the only thing any machine can do is what a human has instructed it to do.

（1） We are told that a high-tech cash register is really just ______.

A.an electric instrument of sight

B.a simple adding machine

C.a way to keep employees honest

D.an expensive piece of window dressing

（2） Grocery store price lists are updated by ______.

A.a scanner

B.a telephone hookup

C.an adding machine

D.an employee

（3） Which of the following describes the main idea of the passage?

A.Computers are stupid and inefficient.

B.Computer errors are basically human errors.

C.Computers can help department stores update the price list.

D.Supermarket price errors are often made through dishonesty.

第三章 法律篇

第一節 文化背景知識補充

《美國獨立宣言》

【中文簡介】

《美國獨立宣言》是北美洲十三個英屬殖民地宣告自大不列顛王國獨立，並宣明此舉正當性的文告。1776年7月4日，本宣言在費城舉行的第二次大陸會議上被批准，之後7月4日被定為美國獨立紀念日。宣言的原件由大陸會議出席代表共同簽署，並永久陳列於美國華盛頓特區的國家檔案與文件署（National Archives and Records Administration）。此宣言為美國最重要的立國文書之一。

傑佛遜起草了《獨立宣言》的第一稿，之後富蘭克林等人又進行了潤色。大陸會議對此稿還進行了長時間的、激烈的辯論，最終作出了重大的修改。在喬治亞和卡羅來納代表們的堅持下，刪去了傑佛遜對英王喬治三世允許在殖民地保持奴隸制和奴隸買賣的有力譴責。這一部分的原文是這樣的：

他對人性本身發動了殘酷的戰爭，侵犯了一個從未冒犯過他的遠方民族的最神聖的生存權和自由權；他誘騙他們，並把他們運往另一半球充當奴隸，還使他們其中一些人慘死在運送途中。

湯瑪斯· 傑佛遜（1743—1826），生於維吉尼亞的一個富裕家庭。曾就讀於威廉一瑪麗學院。1767年成為律師，1769年當選為弗吉尼亞下院議議員。他積極投身於獨立運動之中，並代表維吉尼亞出席大陸會議。他曾兩次當選維吉尼亞州州長。1800年當選美國總統。

傑佛遜在自己的墓誌銘中這樣寫道：

這裡埋葬著湯瑪斯·傑佛遜，美國《獨立宣言》的作者，維吉尼亞宗教自由法規的制定者和維吉尼亞大學之父。

起草《獨立宣言》的場景

【《獨立宣言》原文】

The Declaration of Independence

IN CONGRESS, JULY 4, 1776

THE UNANIMOUS DECLARATION OF

THE THIRTEEN UNITED STATES OF AMERAICA

When in the course of human events it becomes necessary for one people to dissolve the political bands which have connected them with another and to assume among the powers of the earth, the separate and equal station to which the Laws of

Nature and of Nature's God entitle them, a decent respect to the opinions of mankind requires that they should declare the causes which impel them to the separation.

We hold these truths to be self-evident, that all men are created equal, that they are endowed by their Creator with certain unalienable Rights, that among these are Life, Liberty and the pursuit of Happiness. That to secure these rights, Governments are instituted among Men, deriving their just powers from the consent of the governed. That whenever any Form of Government becomes destructive of these ends, it is the Right of the People to alter or to abolish it, and to institute new Government, laying its foundation on such principles and organizing its powers in such form, as to them shall seem most likely to effect their Safety and Happiness. Prudence, indeed, will dictate that Governments long established should not be changed for light and transient causes; and accordingly all experience hath shewn, that mankind are more disposed to suffer, while evils are sufferable, than to right themselves by abolishing the forms to which they are accustomed. But when a long train of abuses and usurpations, pursuing invariably the same Object evinces a design to reduce them under absolute Despotism, it is their right, it is their duty, to throw off such Government, and to provide new Guards for their future security. Such has been the patient sufferance of these Colonies; and such is now the necessity which constrains them to alter their former Systems of Government. The history of the present King of Great Britain is a history of repeated injuries and usurpations, all having in direct object the establishment of an absolute Tyranny over these States. To prove this, let Facts be submitted to a candid world.

He has refused his Assent to laws, the most wholesome and necessary for the public good.

He has forbidden his Governors to pass Laws of immediate and pressing importance, unless suspended in their operation till his Assent should be obtained;

and when so suspended, he has utterly neglected to attend to them.

He has refused to pass other Laws for the accommodation of large districts of people, unless those people would relinquish the right of Representation in the Legislature, a right inestimable to them and formidable to tyrants only.

He has called together legislative bodies at places unusual, uncomfortable, and distant from the depository of their public Records, for the sole purpose of fatiguing them into compliance with his measures.

He has dissolved Representative Houses repeatedly, for opposing with manly firmness his invasions on the rights of the people.

He has refused for a long time, after such dissolutions, to cause others to be elected; whereby the Legislative powers, incapable of Annihilation, have returned to the People at large for their exercise; the State remaining in the mean time exposed to all the dangers of invasion from without, and convulsions within.

He has endeavored to prevent the population of these States; for that purpose obstructing the Laws for Naturalization of Foreigners; refusing to pass others to encourage their migrations hither, and raising the conditions of new Appropriations of lands.

He has obstructed the Administration of Justice, by refusing his Assent of Laws for establishing Judiciary powers.

He has made Judges dependent on his Will alone, for the tenure of their offices, and the amount and payment of their salaries.

He has erected a multitude of New Offices, and sent hither swarms of Officers to harass our people, and eat out their substance.

He has kept among us, in times of peace, Standing Armies without the Consent of our legislatures.

He has affected to render the Military independent of and superior to the Civil power.

He has combined with others to subject us to a jurisdiction foreign to our constitution, and unacknowledged by our laws; giving his Assent to their Acts of pretended Legislation:

For Quartering large bodies of armed troops among us;

For protecting them, by a mock Trial, from punishment for any Murders which they should commit on the inhabitants of these States;

For cutting off our Trade with all parts of the world;

For imposing Taxes on us without our Consent;

For depriving us in many cases, of the benefits of Trial by Jury;

For transporting us beyond Seas to be tried for pretended offenses;

For abolishing the free System of English Laws in a neighboring Province, establishing therein an Arbitrary government, and enlarging its Boundaries so as to render it at once an example and fit instrument for introducing the same absolute rule into these Colonies;

For taking away our Charters, abolishing our most valuable Laws, and altering fundamentally the Forms of our Governments;

For suspending our own Legislatures, and declaring themselves invested with power to legislate for us in all cases whatsoever.

He has abdicated Government here, by declaring us out of his Protection and waging War against us.

He has plundered our seas, ravaged our Coasts, burnt our towns, and destroyed the lives of our people.

He is at this time transporting large Armies of foreign Mercenaries to compleat the works of death, desolation and tyranny, already begun with circumstances of Cruelty and Perfidy scarcely paralleled in the most barbarous ages, and totally unworthy the Head of a civilized nation.

He has constrained our fellow Citizens taken Captive on the high Seas to bear Arms against their Country, to become the executioners of their friends and Brethren, or to fall themselves by their Hands.

He has excited domestic insurrections amongst us, and has endeavored to bring on the inhabitants of our frontiers, the merciless Indian Savages, whose known rule of warfare, is an undistinguished destruction of all ages, sexes, and conditions.

In every stage of these Oppressions We have Petitioned for Redress in the most humble terms: Our repeated Petitions have been answered only by repeated injury. A Prince whose character is thus marked by every act which may define a Tyrant, is unfit to be the ruler of a free people.

Nor have We been wanting in attentions to our British brethren. We have warned them from time to time of attempts by their legislature to extend an unwarrantable jurisdiction over us. We have reminded them of the circumstances of our emigration and settlement here. We have appealed to their native justice and magnanimity, and we have conjured them by the ties of our common kindred to disavow these usurpations, which, would inevitably interrupt our connections and correspondence. They too have been deaf to the voice of justice and of consanguinity. We must, therefore, acquiesce in the necessity, which denounces our Separation, and hold them, as we hold the rest of mankind, Enemies in War, in Peace Friends.

We, therefore, the Representatives of the united States of America, in General Congress, assembled, appealing to the supreme Judge of the world for the rectitude of our intentions, do, in the Name, and by Authority of the good People of these Colonies, solemnly publish and declare, That these United Colonies are, and of

Right ought to be Free and Independent States; that they are Absolved from all Allegiance to the British Crown, and that all political connection between them and the State of Great Britain, is and ought to be totally dissolved; and that as Free and Independent States, they have full Power to Levy War, conclude Peace, contract Alliances, establish Commerce, and to do all other Acts and Things which Independent States may of right do. And for the support of this Declaration, with a firm reliance on the protection of Divine Providence, we mutually pledge to each other our Lives, our Fortunes, and our sacred Honor.

【中文譯文】

在人類事務發展的過程中，當一個民族必須解除同另一個民族的聯繫，並按照自然法則和上帝的旨意，以獨立平等的身分立於世界列國之林時，出於對人類輿論的尊重，必須把驅使他們獨立的原因予以宣布。

我們認為下述真理是不言而喻的：人人生而平等，造物主賦予他們若干不可剝奪的權利，其中包括生存權、自由權和追求幸福的權利。為了保障這些權利，人們才在他們中間建立政府，而政府的正當權利，則是經被統治者同意並授予的。任何形式的政府一旦對這些目標的實現起了破壞作用，人民便有權予以更換或廢除，以建立一個新的政府。新政府所依據的原則和組織其權利的方式，務使人民認為唯有這樣才最有可能使他們獲得安全和幸福。若真要審慎地來說，成立多年的政府是不應當由於無關緊要的和一時的原因而予以更換的。過去的一切經驗都說明，任何苦難，只要尚能忍受的，人類還是情願忍受的，也不想為了自身權益而廢除他們久已習慣了的政府形式。然而，當始終追求同一目標的一系列濫用職權和強取豪奪的行為表明政府企圖把人民置於專制暴政之下時，人民就有權也有義務去推翻這樣的政府，並為其未來的安全提供新的保障。這就是這些殖民地過去忍受苦難的經過，也是他們現在不得不改變政府制度的原因。當今大不列顛王國的歷史，就是屢屢傷害和掠奪這些殖民地的歷史，其直接目標就是要在各州之上建立一個獨裁暴政。為了證明上述句句屬實，現將事實公之於世，讓公正的世人作出評判。

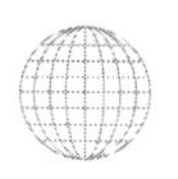

他拒絕批准對公眾利益最有益、最必需的法律。

他禁止他的殖民總督批准刻不容緩、極端重要的法律，要不就先行擱置等候他的同意，而這些法律被擱置以後，他又完全置之不理。

他拒絕批准便利廣大地區人民的其他的法律，除非這些地區的人民情願放棄自己在立法機構中的代表權；而代表權對人民是無比珍貴的，只有暴君才畏懼這種權利。

他把各州的立法委員召集到一個異乎尋常、極不舒適而又遠離他們的檔案庫的地方去開會，其目的無非是使他們疲憊不堪，被迫就範。

他一再解散各州的眾議院，因為眾議院堅決反對他侵犯人民的權利。

他在解散眾議院之後，又長期拒絕另選新議會，於是這項不可剝奪的立法權便歸由人民來行使，致使在這期間各州仍處於外敵入侵和內部騷亂的種種危險之中。

他竭力阻止各州增加人口，為此目的，他阻撓外國人入籍法的通過，拒絕批准其他鼓勵移民的法律，並提高分配新土地的條件。

他拒絕批准建立司法權的法律，以阻撓司法的執行。

他迫使法官為了保住職位和薪金而置於他個人意志的支配之下。

他濫設新官署，委派大批官員到這裡騷擾我們的人民，吞噬他們的財物。

他在和平時期，未經我們立法機構同意，就在我們這裡維持其常備軍。

他施加影響，使軍隊獨立於民政之外，並凌駕於民政之上。

他同他人勾結，把我們置於一種既不符合我們的法規也未經我們法律承認的管轄之下，而且還批准他們炮製各種偽法案，以便達到以下目的：在我們中間駐紮大批武裝部隊；不論這些人對我們各州居民犯下何等嚴重的罪行，都可用假審判來庇護他們，讓他們逍遙法外；切斷我們同世界各地的貿易；未經我們同意便向我們強行徵稅；在許多案件中剝奪我們享有陪審制的權益；以莫須有的罪名把我們押送海外受審；在一個鄰省廢除了英國的自由法制，在那裡建立專制政府，

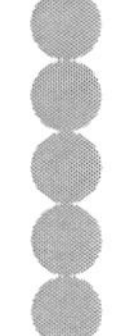

擴大其疆域，使其立即成為一個樣板和合適的工具，以便向這裡各殖民地推行同樣的專制統治；取消我們的憲章，廢除我們最珍貴的法律並從根本上改變我們各州政府的形式；終止我們立法機構行使權力，宣稱他們自己擁有在任何情況下為我們制定法律的權力。

他們放棄設在這裡的政府，宣稱我們已不屬他們保護之列，並向我們發動戰爭。

他在我們的海域裡大肆掠奪，蹂躪我們的沿海地區，燒毀我們的城鎮，殘害我們人民的生命。

他此時正在運送大批外國僱傭兵來從事其製造死亡、荒涼和暴政的勾當，其殘忍與卑劣從一開始就連最野蠻的時代也難以相比，他已完全不配當一個文明國家的元首。

他強迫我們在公海被他們俘虜的同胞拿起武器反對自己的國家，使他們成為殘殺自己親友的劊子手，或者死於自己親友的手下。

他在我們中間煽動內亂，並竭力調唆殘酷無情的印第安人來對付我們邊疆的居民，而眾所周知，印第安人作戰的準則是不分男女老幼、是非曲直，格殺勿論。

在遭受這些壓迫的每一階段，我們都曾以最謙卑的言辭請其予以糾正。而我們一次又一次的請願換來的卻是一次又一次的傷害。一個君主，當他的品格已被打上了暴君的烙印時，就不配君臨自由的人民。

我們並不是沒有想到我們英國的弟兄。他們的立法機關想把無理的管轄權擴展到我們這裡來，我們也時常向他們提醒過此事。我們也曾把我們移民來這裡、定居在這裡的情況告訴他們。我們曾向他們呼籲天生的正義感和雅量，希望念在同種同宗的分上，拒絕這些掠奪行為，以免其不可避免地影響到我們之間的關係和來往。可他們對這種正義和同宗的呼聲也同樣充耳不聞。因此，我們不得不宣布脫離他們，以對待世界上其他民族的態度對待他們：跟我交戰者，就是敵人；跟我友好者，即為朋友。

因此我們這些在大陸會議上集會的美利堅合眾國的代表們，以各殖民地善良人民的名義，並經他們授權，向世界最高裁判者申訴，說明我們的嚴正意向，同時鄭重宣布：

我們這些聯合起來的殖民地現在是，而且按理也應該是，獨立自由的國家；我們對英國王室效忠的全部義務結束了，我們與大不列顛王國之間的一切政治聯繫全部斷絕，而且必須斷絕。

作為一個獨立自主的國家，我們完全有權宣戰、締和、結盟、通商，並採取獨立國家有權採取的一切行動。

我們堅決信賴上帝的保佑，同時以我們的生命、財產和神聖的名譽彼此宣誓來支持這一宣言。

第二節 相關知識連結

三權分立

【中文簡介】

三權分立（Checks and Balances），亦稱三權分治，是西方資本主義國家的基本政治制度的建制原則。其核心是，立法權、行政權和司法權相互獨立、互相制衡。三權分立具體到做法上，即為行政、司法、立法三大權力分屬三個地位相等的不同政府機構，由三者互相制衡。是當前世界上資本主義民主國家廣泛採用的一種民主政治思想。

英國著名政治學家洛克最早在17世紀提出行政、立法的兩權分立，用以鞏固當時英國的資產階級革命成果。後來該學說不斷傳播，並被法國著名啟蒙思想家、法學家孟德斯鳩詮釋為行政、立法、司法三權分立的形式，解決了在該種政治制度下可能出現的部分問題。該學說在當時被廣泛認為是民主制度的有力保證。

這一學說基於這樣一個理論前提，即絕對的權力導致絕對的腐敗，所以，國

家權力應該分立，互相制衡。資產階級的思想家們希望據此建立一個民主、法治的國家。英法資產階級革命和美國獨立戰爭以後，三權分立成為資產階級建立國家制度的根本原則。在當代，儘管西方國家的政治制度發生了很大變化，但三權分立仍然是它的一個根本特點。

分權的目的在於避免獨裁者的產生。古代的皇帝以至地方官員均集立法、執法（行政）、司法三大權於一身，容易造成權力的濫用。在現代，立法、運用稅款的權力通常掌握在代表人民意願的議會手中，司法權的獨立在於防止執法機構濫權。

【英文簡介】

Legislative Branch-represented by Congress, includes two parts: the House of Representatives and the Senate. Congress meets in Washington, D.C., and both branches study bills which will become future laws and problems which affect the nation.

The House of Representatives, whose 435 members are elected according to the population of each state, includes the Speaker of the House (the head of the majority party) who becomes president if both the president and vice-president die or become incapacitated. Representatives are elected for two year terms.

The senate, which consists of two members from each state and the members are elected for terms of six years. The senators help create and pass laws, and also interview candidates that the president elects for certain offices (such as Supreme Court justices). It can also ratify treaties the president makes (with a 2/3 majority).

Executive Branch-represented by the President. The Electoral College chooses the president based on a state's popular vote. When the majority of a state's citizens vote for a candidate, then that state's electors vote for the new president.

The President must be born a citizen of the United States, and must be at least 35 years old by the time he will assume his office. He has important duties, including the role of commander-in-chief of the armed forces, and negotiating treaties with other countries. He also must sign bills that are passed in Congress (and can veto those he doesn't approve). The President also represents America around the world when he meets with the leaders of other governments. The President's job is complex, so he appoints a Cabinet with members who help him lead the nation. Congress must approve his appointments.

Judicial Branch-represented by Supreme Court. The American judicial system is composed of courts, judge, jurors, lawyers, spectators, and rules.

In 1787, the Constitution of the new nation created the Judicial Branch of government, which the Supreme Court represents. It has grown from six justices to nine, which include one chief justice and eight associates who are appointed for a lifetime term by the president of the United States.

The Supreme Court is the highest court of law in the United States, and is over other federal courts such as the Court of Appeals, District Courts, and Special Courts. The role of the Supreme Court is to interpret the Constitution, and to rule in any cases that involve foreign dignitaries or a state. A majority of even one vote will pass a judgment that becomes a role model for future similar decisions in courts around the nation.

【詞彙】

legislative adj. 立法的，立法機關的

senate n. 參議院，上院

incapacitated adj. 喪失勞動能力的

majority n. 多數，大半，〔律〕成年

negotiate v. （與某人）商議，談判，磋商，買賣，讓渡（支票、債券等），通過，越過

veto n. 否決，禁止，否決權 vt. 否決，禁止

cabinet n. （有抽屜或格子的）櫥櫃，<美>內閣

judicial adj. 司法的，法院的，公正的，明斷的

federal adj. 聯邦的，聯合的，聯邦制的，同盟的

dignitaries n. 權貴，高官，高僧，（尤指教會中）顯要人物

【問題】

1.What are the three branches and by whom are they represented respectively?

2.What are the president's important duties?

第三節 練習

1.Match the synonymic phrases.

A.commit a.to tell someone not to punish a person too severely

B.convict b.to initiate civil or criminal court action against an offense or crime, especially by the verdict of a court

C.deter c.nevertheless, in spite of that, however

D.nonetheless d.to discourage, to hinder from

E.prosecute e.to find or prove (someone) guilty

F.be/go easy on sb/sth f.to perform (a crime, foolish act etc.)

2.Translate the following sentences into English.

（1）我們如果不理解這一點，就會犯極大的錯誤。

（2）他被託付給一個姨媽照顧。

（3）誰也不肯負責作出明確的答覆。

（4）我們答應過要幫助他們。

（5）他對你所説的事表示懷疑，但他是服理的。（如果你説得有道理，他還是會相信的。）

（6）我堅信這情形將會改善。

（7）他的論點對西方讀者沒有什麼説服力。

3.Paraphrase. Tell the meanings of the following sentences in your own words.

（1） Each year almost a third of the households in America are victims of violence or theft.

（2） This is why the certainty and severity of punishment must go down when the crime rate goes up.

（3） A decade of careful research has failed to provide clear and convincing evidence that the threat of punishment reduces crime.

（4） While elite colleges and universities still have high standards of admissions, some of the most "exclusive" prisons now require about five prior serious crimes before an inmate is accepted into their correctional program.

（5） The first-year operating cost would be＄150,000 per crime prevented, worth it if the victim were you or me, but much too expensive to be feasible as a national policy.

4.Cloze. Fill in the blanks according to the text: More Crimes and Less Punishment

A few （1）from the Justice Department's recent "Report to the Nation on Crime and Justice"（2）my point. Of every 100 serious crimes （3）in America, only 33 are actually reported to the police. Of the 33 reported, about six lead to arrest. Of the six arrested, only three are （4）and convicted. The others are rejected or （5）due to evidence or witness problems or sent elsewhere for medical treatment instead of punishment. Of the three convicted, only one is sent to prison. The other two are allowed to live in their community under （6）. Of the select few sent to prison, more than half receive a （7）sentence of five years. The average（8）, however, leave prison in about two years. Most prisoners gain early （9）not because （10）boards are too easy on crime, but because it is much cheaper to supervise a criminal in the community.

5.Complete each of the following sentences with the most likely answer.

（1） Mr.Wells, together with all the members of his family, ______for Europe this afternoon.

A.are to leave B.are leaving C.is leaving D.leave

（2） It was suggested that all government ministers should______information on their financial interests.

A.discover B.uncover C.tell D.disclose

（3） As my exams are coming next week, I'll take advantage of the weekend to______on some reading.

A.catch up B.clear up C.make up D.pick up

（4） I'm surprised they are no longer on speaking terms. It's not like either of them to bear a______.

A.disgust B.curse C.grudge D.hatred

（5） Mary hopes to be______from hospital next week.

A.dismissed B.discharged C.expelled D.resigned

（6） Once a picture is proved to be a forgery, it becomes quite______.

A.invaluable B.priceless C.unworthy D.worthless

（7） Jimmy earns his living by______works of art in the museum.

A.recovering B.restoring C.renewing D.reviving

（8） I couldn't sleep last night because the tap in the bathroom was______.

A.draining B.dropping C.spilling D.dripping

（9） The book gives a brief______of the course of his research up till now.

A.outline B.reference C.frame D.outlook

（10） She was sanding outside in the snow, ______with cold.

A.spinning B.shivering C.shaking D.staggering

6.Reading comprehension.

Every year thousands of people are arrested and taken to court for shop-lifting.In Britain alone, about HK ＄3,000,000's worth of goods are stolen from shops every week. This amounts to something like HK＄150 million a year, and represents about 4 per cent of the shops' total stock. As a result of this "shrinkage" as the shops call it, the honest public has to pay higher prices.

Shop-lifters can be divided into three main categories: the professionals, the deliberate amateur, and the people who just can't help themselves. The professionals do not pose much of a problem for the store detectives, who, assisted by closed circuit television, two-way mirrors and various other technological devices, can usually cope with them. The professionals tend to go for high value goods in parts of the shops where security measures are tightest. And, in any case, they account for only a small percentage of the total losses due to shop-lifting.

The same applies to the deliberate amateur who is, so to speak, a professional in training. Most of them get caught sooner or later, and they are dealt with severely by the courts.

The real problem is the person who gives way to a sudden temptation and is in all other respects an honest and law-abiding citizen.Contrary to what one would expect, this kind of shop-lifter is rarely poor. He does not steal because he needs the goods and cannot afford to pay for them.He steals because he simply cannot stop himself. And there are countless others who, because of age, sickness or plain absent-mindedness, simply forget to pay for what they take from the shops. When caught, all are liable to prosecution and the decision whether to send for the police or not is in the hands of the store manager.

In order to prevent the quite incredible growth in ship-lifting offences, some stores, in fact, are doing their best to separate the thieves from the confused by prohibiting customers from taking bags into the store. However, what is most worrying about the whole problem is, perhaps, that it is yet another instance of the innocent majority being penalized and inconvenienced because of the actions of a small minority. It is the aircraft hijack situation in another form. Because of the possibility of one passenger in a million boarding an aircraft with a weapon, the other 999,999 passengers must subject themselves to searches and delays. Unless the situation in the shops improves, in ten years' time we may all have to subject ourselves to a body-search every time we go into a store to buy a tin of beans!

(1) Why does the honest public have to pay higher prices when they go to the shops? ______

A.There is "shrinkage" in market values.

B.Many goods are not available.

C.Goods in many shops lack variety.

D.There are many cases of shop-lifting.

(2) The third group of people steal things because they______

A.are mentally ill. B.are quite absent-minded.

C.can not resist the temptation. D.can not afford to pay for goods.

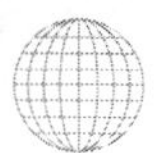

（3） According to the passage, law-abiding citizens _______.

A.can possibly steal things because of their poverty

B.can possibly take away goods without paying

C.have never stolen goods from the supermarkets

D.are difficult to be caught when they steal things

（4） Which of the following statements is NOT true about the main types of shoplifting? _______

A.A big percentage of the total losses are caused by the professionals.

B.The deliberate amateurs will be punished severely if they get caught.

C.People would expect that those who can't help themselves are poor.

D.The professionals don't cause a lot of trouble to the store detectives.

（5） The aircraft hijack situation is used in order to show that _______.

A."the professionals do not pose much of a problem for the stores"

B.some people "simply forget to pay for what they take from the shops"

C."the innocent majority are inconvenienced because of the actions of a small minority"

D.the third type of shop-lifters are dangerous people

第四章 教育篇

第一節 文化背景知識補充

一、哥倫比亞大學

【中文簡介】

哥倫比亞大學（Columbia University）是美國最古老的五所大學之一。這裡的學生在聯合國學政治，在華爾街讀金融，在百老匯看戲劇，在林肯中心聽音樂。歐元之父孟岱爾在這裡留下光輝的足跡，基因學的奠基人摩爾根在這裡掀起生物界最徹底的革命！美國新聞界至高無上的普立茲獎在這裡誕生。這裡擁有美國第一所授予博士學位的醫學院。美國前總統羅斯福，聯合國前祕書長加林曾在這裡求學，中國的聞一多、徐志摩、李政道等著名學者在這裡留下了青春的腳步。250年來科學與藝術是它永恆不變的主題！

哥倫比亞大學是世界上最具聲望的高等學府之一。它位於美國紐約市曼哈頓的晨邊高地，瀕臨哈德遜河，在中央公園北面。它於1754 年根據英國國王喬治二世頒布的《國王憲章》而成立，命名為國王學院，是美洲大陸最古老的學院之一。美國獨立戰爭後為紀念發現美洲大陸的哥倫布而更名為哥倫比亞學院，1896年改為哥倫比亞大學。

哥倫比亞大學屬於私立的常春藤盟校，由三個本科生院和十三個研究生院構成。現有教授三千多人，學生兩萬餘人，校友25萬人遍布世界150多個國家。學校每年經費預算約20億美元，圖書館藏書870萬冊。哥倫比亞學院是美國最早進行通才教育的本科生院，至今仍保持著美國大學中最嚴格的核心課程。它的研究生院更是以卓越的學術成就而聞名。整個20世紀上半葉，哥倫比亞大學和哈佛大學及芝加哥大學一起被公認為美國高等教育的三強。至2007年，哥倫比亞的校友和教授中一共有87人獲得過諾貝爾獎。此外，學校的醫學、法學、商學和新聞學都名列前茅。其新聞學院頒發的普立茲獎是美國文學和新聞界的最高榮譽。

【英文簡介】

Columbia University in the City of New York, is a private university in the United States and a member of the Ivy League. Columbia's main campus lies in the Morningside Heights neighborhood in the borough of Manhattan, in New York City. The institution was established as King's College by the Church of England, receiving a Royal Charter in 1754 from George Ⅱ of the Great Britain. One of only two universities in the United States to have been founded by royal charter (the other being the College of William &Mary), it was the fifth college established in the State Colonies and the only college established in the State of New York.After the American Revolutionary War, it was briefly chartered as a New York State entity from 1784 -1787. The university now operates under a 1787 charter that places the institution under a private board of trustees. Columbia annually grants the Pulitzer Prizes, and more Nobel Prize winners are affiliated with Columbia than with any other institution in the world.

富蘭克林· 羅斯福

西奧多· 羅斯福

Three United States Presidents, nine Justices of the Supreme Court of the United States and 39 Nobel Prize winners have studied at Columbia. Alumni also have received more than 20 National Book Awards and 95 Pulitzer Prizes. Four United States Poet Laureates received their degrees from Columbia. Today, three United States Senators and 16 current Chief Executives of Fortune 500 companies hold Columbia degrees, as do seven of the 25 richest Americans. Alumni of the University have served (in more than 70 positions) as members of U.S. Presidential Cabinets or as U.S. Presidential advisers. More than 40 U.S. senators, 90 U.S. congresspersons, and 35 U.S. governors have received their education at Columbia. Alumni have founded or been the president of more than fifty-five universities and colleges in the nation and the world.

Barack Obama, President of the US, Columbia College

Franklin Delano Roosevelt, President of the US, Columbia Law School

Theodore Roosevelt, President of the US, Columbia Law School

【詞彙】

affiliated	adj.	附屬的
alumni	n.	校友（複數）
Charter	n.	憲章
colony	n.	殖民地
entity	n.	實體
supreme	adj.	最高的
undergraduate	adj.	本科的

【問題】

1.Which prize does Columbia University annually grant?

2.How many presidents have graduated from Columbia University and who are they?

二、普立茲獎

【中文簡介】

普立茲獎也稱為普立茲新聞獎。1917 年根據美國報業巨頭約瑟夫· 普立茲（Joseph Pulitzer）的遺願設立，1970、1980年代已經發展成為美國新聞界的一項最高榮譽獎，現在，不斷完善的評選制度已使普立茲獎成為一個全球性的獎項。普立茲獎在每年春季由哥倫比亞大學的普立茲獎評選委員會的14名會員評定，5月由哥倫比亞大學校長正式頒發。

普立茲獎分為兩類：新聞界和創作界。普立茲獎也是一個鼓勵美國的獎項。新聞界的獲獎者可以是任何國籍，但是獲獎作品必須在美國週報（或日報）中發表。創作界除歷史獎外，獲得者必須是美國公民。只要是關於美國歷史的書都可獲獎，作者不必是美國人。

普立茲獎的相關歷史

普立茲生前立下遺囑，將財產捐贈給哥倫比亞大學，設立普立茲獎，獎勵新聞界、文學界、音樂界的卓越人士，該獎自1917年以來每年頒發一次。

1985年來，普立茲獎象徵了美國最負責任的寫作和最優美的文字。特別是新聞獎，更是美國報界的最高榮譽。每一個希望有所作為的美國記者無不以獲得普立茲新聞獎為奮鬥的目標。普立茲獎的評委由有成就的名記者組成。當年的優勝者由評委審查、挑選，但評選結果須經哥倫比亞大學顧問委員會通過，並由哥倫比亞大學校長宣布。

首屆普立茲攝影獎是1942年頒發的。此後，除1946年外，每年頒發一次。從1968年開始，攝影類增設了專題新聞攝影獎，獲獎作品通常由一組照片組成。攝影獎獲獎作品具有重要意義。

普立茲文學獎歷來被美國作家視為一種榮譽。

普立茲的傳奇人生

普立茲（1847年4月10 日—1911 年10 月29 日）生於匈牙利一個猶太人家庭。1864年到美國參加林肯騎兵部隊。一年後退伍，到聖路易城做雜工，自學法律。1867年取得律師資格，同年3 月入美國國籍。1868 年任德文《西方郵報》記者。1869年12月當選密蘇里州眾議員。1876至1877年任《紐約太陽報》駐華盛頓記者。1878年購得《聖路易電訊報》，1880年將它與《晚郵報》合併為《郵報—電訊報》，成為獲利最豐厚的晚報。1883 年買下紐約《世界報》。1884 年當選國會議員，數月後即辭職，專心辦報。1887 年又出版《世界報晚刊》。他採用編輯寫作制——記者採寫的材料由編輯潤色、整理、綜合成稿見報。這種寫作規則至今仍是整個新聞界的普遍原則。他強調新聞的真實、準確，文字簡潔通俗，重視社論，被認為是19世紀70至80年代興起的「新新聞事業」的創始人。1890年辭去《世界報》主編職務。晚年雙目失明。1911年10月29

日，普立茲逝世。遺囑要求捐贈200萬美元作為創建哥倫比亞大學新聞學院（1912 年開辦）的基金，並贈款設立普立茲獎。

【英文簡介】

The Pulitzer Prize is a US award for achievements in newspaper journalism, literature and musical composition. It was established by Joseph Pulitzer and is administered by Columbia University in New York City.

Prizes are awarded yearly in twenty-one categories. In twenty of these, each winner receives a certificate and a US＄10,000 cash award. The winner in the public service category of the journalism competition is awarded a gold medal, which always goes to a newspaper, although an individual may be named in the citation.

The prize was established by Joseph Pulitzer, a journalist and newspaper publisher, who founded the St. Louis Post-Dispatch and bought the New York World; his competition with William Randolph Hearst in New York City led to a set of practices that came to be known as yellow journalism.

Pulitzer left money to Columbia University upon his death in 1911. A portion of his bequest was used to found the university's journalism school in 1912. The first Pulitzer Prizes were awarded on June 4, 1917, and they are now announced each April. Recipients are chosen by an independent board.

【詞彙】

award	v.	授予獎項
bequest	n.	遺贈
board	n.	董事會
category	n.	目錄，類別
certificate	n.	證明，證書

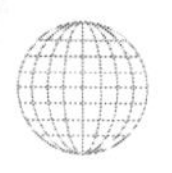

citation n. 引用

portion n. 部分

recipient n. 接受者

【問題】

1.What is Pulitzer Prize?

2.Who is Joseph Pulitzer?

3.How was Pulitzer Prize founded?

第二節 相關知識連結

一、牛津大學

【中文簡介】

英國牛津大學建於1167年，在英國社會和高等教育系統中具有極其重要的地位，也有著世界性的影響。英國甚至全世界教育界，言必稱牛津；英國和世界很多的青年學子們都以進牛津為理想。

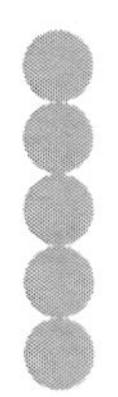

牛津大學

19世紀以前的英國，僅有牛津和劍橋兩所大學，而劍橋大學也是13世紀初由牛津的部分師生創辦的。在歷史上，許多著名的人物都曾就讀於牛津，其中包括4位英國國王、46位諾貝爾獎獲得者、25位英國首相、3位聖人、86位大主教以及18位紅衣主教。

瑪格麗特· 柴契爾：1943年進入牛津大學薩默維爾女子學院攻讀化學。大學時代參加保守黨，並擔任牛津大學保守黨協會主席。曾4次訪問中國，1984年在北京代表英國政府與中國政府簽署了《中英關於香港問題的聯合聲明》，為香港回歸中國奠定了堅實的政治基礎。

東尼· 布萊爾：畢業於牛津大學聖約翰學院法律系，1997年5月任首相，成為自1812年以來英國最年輕的首相，後兼任首席財政大臣和文官部大臣。2001年6月在大選中再次獲勝，連任首相，成為英國歷史上首位連任的工黨首相。

比爾‧柯林頓：出身貧寒的柯林頓在喬治城大學外交學院拿到國際關係學位後，又獲得了羅德獎學金，得以到英國牛津大學深造。曾經擔任過美國第42任總統，長達8年。到2001年離職時，柯林頓是歷史上得到公眾肯定最多的總統之一。

T.S.艾略特：1906年進入哈佛大學學哲學，續而到英國上牛津大學，後留英教書和當職員。1908年開始創作。有詩集《普魯弗洛克及其他觀察到的事物》、《詩選》、《四個四重奏》等。代表作為長詩《荒原》，表達了西方一代人精神上的幻滅，被認為是西方現代文學中具有劃時代意義的作品。1948年因「革新現代詩，功績卓著的先驅」，獲諾貝爾獎文學獎。

史蒂芬‧霍金：1942年1月8日在英國牛津出生，曾先後畢業於牛津大學和劍橋大學三一學院，並獲劍橋大學哲學博士學位。英國劍橋大學應用數學及理論物理學系教授，當代最重要的廣義相對論和宇宙論家，是20世紀享有國際盛譽的偉人之一，被稱為在世的最偉大的科學家，還被稱為「宇宙之王」。

牛津大學各學院學生總數有一萬兩千人左右，其中九千名左右是大學部學生，而教職員共有五千四百人。大學中的主要行政人員均選自牛津本身的教授及研究員。校長（Chancellor）是一個名譽職位，是學校的最高層人物，主持學校的主要儀式。實際行政工作由學校每四年任命一位「副校長」（Vice-Chancellor）管理，他掌管著學校政務會——一個由選舉出來的教職員工組成的負責學校日常事務的組織。大學的學術性事務則由總董事會管理，總董事會的主席每兩年選舉一次。

【英文簡介】

The University of Oxford (informally Oxford University, or simply Oxford), located in the City of Oxford, Oxfordshire, Great Britain, is the oldest university in the English-speaking world. It is also regarded as one of the world's leading academic institutions and best university in the UK according to all recent league tables of British universities. The name is sometimes abbreviated as Oxon in post-nominals (from the Latin Oxoniensis), although Oxf is sometimes used in official

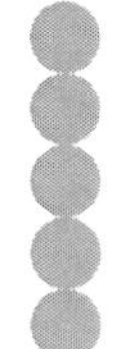

publications. The University has 38 independent colleges and six permanent private halls.

The university traces its roots back to at least 1167, although the exact date of foundation remains unclear, and there is evidence of teaching there as far back as the 10th century. After a dispute between students and townsfolk broke out in 1209, some of the academics at Oxford fled north-east to the town of Cambridge, where the University of Cambridge was founded. The two universities (collectively known as "Oxbridge") have since had a long history of competition with each other.

劍橋大學

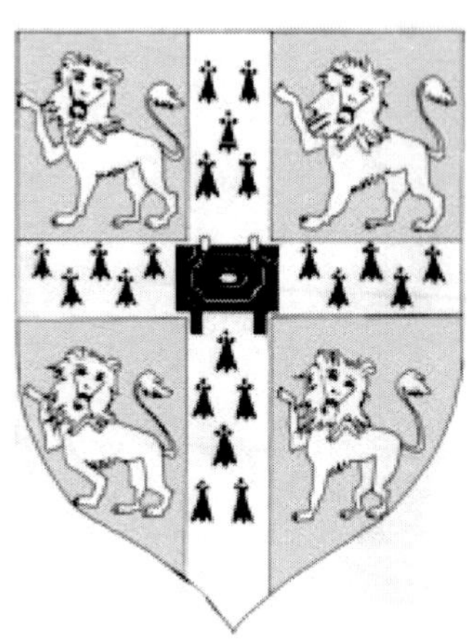

劍橋大學校徽

There are many famous Oxonians (as alumni of the University are known). Twenty-five British prime ministers have attended Oxford (including Margaret Thatcher and Tony Blair). At least twenty-five other international leaders have been educated at Oxford. This number includes three Prime Ministers of Australia, two Prime Ministers of India (Manmohan Singh and Indira Gandhi) and Bill Clinton, the first President of the United States to have attended Oxford (he attended as a Rhodes Scholar). The Burmese democracy activist and Nobel laureate, Aung San Suu Kyi, was a student of St. Hugh's College. Forty-seven Nobel prize-winners have studied or taught at Oxford.

The university's formal head is the Chancellor, though as with most British universities, the Chancellor is a titular figure, rather than someone involved with the day-to-day running of the university. The Chancellor is elected by the members of Convocation, a body comprising all graduates of the university, and holds office until death.

The Vice-Chancellor is the "de facto" head of the University. Five Pro-Vice Chancellors have specific responsibilities for Education, Research, Planning and

Resources, Development and External Affairs, and Personnel and Equal Opportunities. The University Council is the executive policy-forming body, which consists of the Vice-Chancellor as well as heads of departments and other members elected by Congregation, in addition to observers from the Student Union.Congregation, the "parliament of the dons", comprises over 3,700 members of the University's academic and administrative staff, and has ultimate responsibility for legislative matters: it discusses and pronounces on policies proposed by the University Council.Oxford and Cambridge (which is similarly structured) are unique for this democratic form of governance.

【詞彙】

abbreviate	v.	縮寫
Chancellor	n.	英國大學校長
Convocation	n.	大學同學會
collectively	adv.	集體的
comprise	v.	包含
dispute	n.	紛爭
titular	adj.	有名無實的，有頭銜的
townsfolk	n.	市民
permanent	adj.	永久的

【問題】

1.Which university is the oldest one in the English-speaking world?

2.What role does Vice Chancellor play in British universities?

3.How was the University of Cambridge founded?

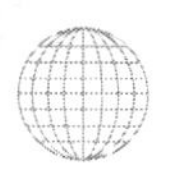

二、哈佛大學

【中文簡介】

在世界各大報刊以及研究機構提供的排行榜上，哈佛大學的排名經常是世界第一。它與世界上第一條地下鐵、第一條電話線生活在同一個城市！美國獨立戰爭以來幾乎所有的革命先驅都出自於它的門下，它被譽為美國政府的思想庫。先後誕生了八位美國總統，四十位諾貝爾獎得主和三十位普立茲獎得主。它的一舉一動決定著美國的社會發展和經濟走向，商學院案例教學盛名遠播。培養了微軟、IBM等一個個商業奇蹟的締造者。它的燕京學社傾力於中美文化的交流。溝通中美兩國關係的基辛格博士，奠基了中國近代人文和自然學科的林語堂、竺可楨、梁實秋、梁思成，一個個響亮的名字，都和這所世界最著名的高等學府息息相關。

哈佛大學校徽

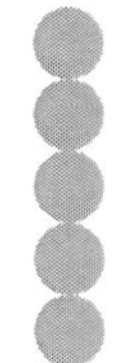

哈佛大學為最早的私立大學之一，以培養研究生和從事科學研究為主。總部位於波士頓的劍橋城，在劍橋城，與哈佛大學相鄰的是與之齊名的麻省理工學院

（MIT）。有趣的是，兩所大學校園之間並沒有明顯的界線。

哈佛大學前身為哈佛學院。1636年10月28日，馬薩諸塞海灣殖民地議會通過決議，決定籌建一所像英國劍橋大學那樣的高等學府，撥款400萬英鎊。由於創始人中不少人出身於英國劍橋大學，他們就把哈佛大學所在的新鎮命名為劍橋。1638年9月14日，牧師約翰· 哈佛病逝，他把自己一半的積蓄779英鎊和400餘冊圖書捐贈給了這所學校。1639年3月13日，馬薩諸塞海灣殖民地議會通過決議，把這所學校命名為哈佛學院。在建校的最初一個半世紀中，學校體制主要仿照歐洲大學。各學院具有相對的獨立性，哈佛曆任校長堅持3A原則，即學術自由、學術自治和學術中立（這三個原則英文詞第一個字母均是A）。

如今，哈佛大學已發展為擁有十個研究生院、四十多個系所、一百多個專業的大型院校。正式註冊有18000名學位候選人，以研究生為主，也包括大學生。

歷史上，哈佛大學的畢業生中共有八位曾當選為美國總統。他們是約翰· 亞當斯、約翰· 昆西· 亞當斯、拉瑟福德· 海斯、西奧多· 羅斯福、富蘭克林· 羅斯福（連任四屆）、約翰· 甘迺迪和巴拉克· 歐巴馬。

學校從未正式加入過某一個特定的教派。一份出版於1643年的早期的小冊子闡明了哈佛大學存在的意義：「促進知識並使之永存後代。」

【英文簡介】

Harvard University is a private university located in Cambridge, Massachusetts, and a member of the Ivy League. Founded in 1636 by the colonial Massachusetts legislature, Harvard is the oldest institution of higher learning in the United States. It is also the first and oldest corporation in North America. Administratively, Harvard comprises ten primary academic units.

Initially called "New College" or "the college at New Town", the institution was renamed Harvard College on March 13, 1639. It was named after a young clergyman named John Harvard, who bequeathed the College his library of four hundred books and£ 779 (which was half of his estate). The earliest known official reference to Harvard as a "university" occurs in the new Massachusetts Constitution of 1780.

During his 40-year tenure as Harvard president (1869-1909), Charles William Eliot radically transformed Harvard into the pattern of the modern research university. Eliot's reforms included elective courses, small classes, and entrance examinations. The Harvard model influenced American education nationally, at both college and secondary levels.

Harvard is consistently ranked at or near the top of international college and university rankings, and has the second-largest financial endowment of any non-profit organization (behind the Bill & Melinda Gates Foundation), standing at $28.8 billion as of 2008. Harvard and Yale have been rivals in academics, rowing, and football for most of their history, competing annually in The Game and the Harvard-Yale Regatta.

Harvard has produced many famous alumni. Among the best-known are American political leaders John Hancock, John Adams, John Quincy Adams, Theodore Roosevelt, Franklin Roosevelt, John F. Kennedy, George W. Bush, and Barack Obama. Seventy-five Nobel Prize winners are affiliated with the university. Since 1974, 19 Nobel Prize winners and 15 winners of the American literary award, the Pulitzer Prize, have served on the Harvard faculty.

【詞彙】

bequeath	v.	遺贈
clergyman	n.	牧師，教士
consistently	adv.	一致地
endowment	n.	捐贈的基金，捐贈
legislature	n.	立法機關

literary adj. 文學的

Massachusetts n. 麻薩諸塞州

rival n. 對手

radically adv. 激進地

tenure n. 任期

【問題】

1.Who is John Harvard?

2.What did Charles William Eliot do during his tenure as Harvard president?

第三節 練習

1.Match the synonymic phrases.

A.all but	a.to become a result
B.to give way to	b.to answer
C.to take in	c.to take action according to
D.in terms of	d.to keep from being damaged
E.to protect sb against sth	e.according to
F.to turn out that	f.to be replaced by
G.to act on	g.to absorb
H.to respond to	h.to eliminate
I.to wipe out	i.almost

2.Translate the following sentences into English.

（1）在那些方面，我接受的教育已經足夠了。

（2）當然，尊重這些差別是十分重要的，但如果只停留於此，就像有了一塊清理好的地面而不知道在上面建什麼。

（3）那個時候，我們大都出於好奇或者為了過一個不同尋常的假期才想到外面的人和地方。

（4）一夜之間世界變小了。那些因偏僻而安靜的遙遠的地區一下子變得熱鬧起來了。

（5）強調表面差異的舊式教育必定要被那種重視相互理解和尊重、重視建立新式公民關係的教育所替代。

3.Paraphrase. Tell the meanings of the following sentences in your own words.

（1） The differences were all but wiped out by the similarities.

（2） For tribalism had persisted from earliest times, though it had taken refined forms.

（3） Remove any one of these and the unity of human needs is attacked and the human race with it.

（4） How to control the engines we have created that threaten to alter the precarious balance on which life depends.

（5） Leadership on this higher level does not require mountains of gold or thundering propaganda.

4.Cloze. Fill in the blanks according to the text: Confessions of a Miseducated Man.

In such an education we begin with the fact （1） the universe itself does not（2）life cheaply. Life is a rare （3）among the millions of （4）and solar system that （5）space. And in this particular solar system life （6）on only one planet. And on that one planet life takes （7）of forms. Of all these （8） forms of life, only one, the human （9），（10）certain faculties in （11） that give it

(12) advantages over all the others. Among those faculties or (13) is a creative (14) that enables man to reflect and (15), to (16) in past experience, and also to (17) future needs. There are endless other wonderful faculties, the workings of (18) are not yet within our understanding—the faculties of hope, (19), appreciation of beauty, (20), love, faith.

5.Complete each of the following sentences with the most likely answer.

(1) He will not be______to vote in this year's election.

A.enough old　　　　B.as old enough

C.old enough　　　　D.enough old as

(2) Thomas Jefferson's achievements as an architect rival his contributions______a politician.

A.such　　　　B.more

C.as　　　　D.than

(3) According to the conditions of my scholarship, after finishing my degree______.

A.my education will be employed by the university

B.employment will be given to me by the university

C.the university will employ me

D.I will be employed by the university

(4) If Bob's wife won't agree to sign the papers, ______.

A.neither he will　　　　B.neither will he

C.neither won't he　　　　D.he won't neither

(5) ______is generally accepted, economic growth is determined by the smooth development of production.

A.What　　B.That

C.It　　D.As

（6） A violent revolution having broken out, all the ports of that country were laid under a(n) ______.

A.boycott　　B.embargo

C.embark　　D.ban

（7） Since______can't work in the United States without a permit, so it is of great importance for them to present their credentials to the government.

A.emigrants　　B.expatriates

C.migrants　　D.immigrants

（8） Most investors are taught at the very beginning that there is no place for______in investment markets.

A.feeling　　B.emotion

C.passion　　D.sentiment

（9） I______my ordinary income by doing some part-time work.

A.compliment　　B.complement

C.supplement　　D.implement

（10） Before the statue could be______to the United States, a site had to be found for it and a pedestal had to be built.

A.transformed　　B.transported

C.transferred　　D.transmitted

6.Reading comprehension.

University teaching in the United Kingdom is very different at both undergraduate and graduate levels from that of many overseas countries.

An undergraduate course consists of a series of lectures, seminars and tutorials and, in science and engineering, laboratory classes, which in total account for about 15 hours per week. Arts students may well find that their official contact with teachers is less than this average, while science and engineering students may expect to be timetabled for up to 20 hours per week. Students studying for a particular degree will take a series of lecture courses which run in parallel at a fixed time in each week and may last one academic term or the whole year. Associated with each lecture course are seminars, tutorials and laboratory classes which draw upon, analyze, illustrate or amplify, the topics presented in the lectures, and lecture classes can vary in size from 20 to 200 although larger sized lectures tend to decrease as students progress into the second and third year and more options become available. Seminars and tutorials are on the whole much smaller than lecture classes and in some departments can be on a one-to-one basis (that is, one member of staff to one student). Students are normally expected to prepare work in advance for seminars and tutorials and this can take the form of researching a topic for discussion, by writing essays or by solving problems. Lectures, seminars and tutorials are all one hour in length, whilst laboratory classes usually last either 2 or 3 hours. Much emphasis is put on how to spend as much time if not more studying by themselves as being taught. In the UK it is still common for people to say that they are 「reading」 for a degree! Each student has a tutor whom they can consult on any matter whether academic or personal. Although the tutor will help, motivation for study is expected to come from the student.

(1) According to the passage, science and engineering courses seem to be more______than arts courses.

A.motivating　　B.varied

C.demanding　　D.interesting

（2） Which of the following is the length of lectures or seminars or tutorials?

A.1 hour B.2 hours

C.3 hours D.15 hours

（3） In British universities teaching and learning are carried out in ______.

A.a variety of ways B.laboratory classes

C.seminars and tutorials D.lectures and tutorials

第五章 宗教篇

第一節 文化背景知識補充

伊甸園

【中文簡介】

造人，是上帝最後的也是最神聖的一項工作。最初的時候，天上尚未降下雨水，地上卻有霧氣蒸騰，滋生植物，滋潤大地。上帝便用泥土造人，在泥坯的鼻中吹入生命的氣息，就創造出了有靈的活人。上帝給他起名叫亞當。但那時的亞當是孤獨的，上帝決心為他造一個配偶，便在他沉睡之際取下他的一根肋骨，又把肉合起來。上帝用這根肋骨造成一個女人，取名叫夏娃。

上帝把夏娃領到亞當跟前，亞當立刻意識到這個女人與自己生命的聯繫，他心中充滿了快慰和滿意，脫口便說：「這是我骨中的骨，肉中的肉啊！可以稱她為女人，因為他是從男人身上取出來的。」男人和女人原本是一體，因此男人和女人長大以後都要離開父母，與對方結合，二人成為一體。

亞當的含義是「人」，夏娃的含義是「生命之母」。他們是中東和西方傳說中人類的生命之初，是人類原始的父親和母親，是人類的始祖。

上帝在東方的伊甸，為亞當和夏娃造了一個樂園。那裡地上撒滿金子、珍珠、紅瑪瑙，各種樹木從地裡長出來，開滿各種奇花異卉，非常好看；樹上的果子還可以作為食物。園子當中還有生命樹和分別善惡樹。還有河水在園中淙淙流淌，滋潤大地。河水分成四道環繞伊甸：第一條河叫比遜，環繞哈胖拉全地；第二條河叫基訓，環繞古實全地；第三條河叫希底結，從亞述旁邊流過；第四條河

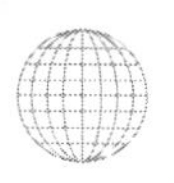

就是伯拉河。作為上帝的恩賜，天不下雨而五穀豐登。

上帝讓亞當和夏娃住在伊甸園中，讓他們修葺並看守這個樂園。上帝吩咐他們說：「園中各樣樹上的果子你們可以隨意吃。只是分別善惡樹上的果子你們不可以吃，吃了的話必死。」

亞當和夏娃赤裸著絕美的形體，品嚐著甘美的果實。他們或款款散步，或悠然躺臥，信口給各種各樣的動植物取名：地上的走獸、天空的飛鳥、園中的嘉樹、田野的鮮花。

他們就這樣在伊甸樂園中幸福地生活著，履行著上帝分配的工作。

最後夏娃受魔鬼（蛇）引誘，不顧上帝的吩咐進食了禁果，又把果子給了亞當，他也吃了。上帝便把他們趕出伊甸園。偷食禁果被認為是人類的原罪及一切其他罪惡的開端。根據魔鬼所說，吃了禁果後，便能如上帝一樣擁有分辨善惡的能力。起初二人赤身裸體，並不知羞恥；吃過禁果後，他們害怕被看見赤身裸體，便拿無花果樹的葉子做衣服。

根據《聖經》，在二人進食禁果後，上帝對蛇、男人及女人有以下的懲罰：蛇「必受詛咒」，從此要用肚子行走並終生吃土；蛇的後裔要與女人的後裔彼此為仇，女人的後裔要傷它們的頭，而蛇的後裔則要傷她們的腳跟；（創3：14—15）女人懷胎的苦楚增加，生產時要受苦；要戀慕丈夫，並被丈夫管轄；（創3：16）男人則要受詛咒，要汗流滿面才得餬口，直到他歸了土；從此需終身勞苦才能從田地裡得到食物，而地裡會長出荊棘和蒺藜（創3：17—19）；為防他們再摘取及進食生命樹的果子以獲永生，便把他們趕出伊甸園；又在伊甸園的東邊安設基路伯及四面轉動會發火焰的劍，以把守前往生命樹的道路。

【英文簡介】

The Garden of Eden is a location described in the Book of Genesis as being the place where the first man, Adam, and his wife, Eve, lived after they were created by God. This garden forms part of the creation myth and theodicy of the Abrahamic religions, and is often used to explain the origin of sin and mankind's wrongdoings.

The creation story in Genesis relates the geographical location of both Eden and the garden to four rivers (Pishon, Gihon, Tigris, Euphrates), and three regions (Havilah, Assyria, and Kush).

Eden's location remains the subject of controversy and speculation among some Christians. There are hypotheses that locate Eden at the headwaters of the Tigris and Euphrates (northern Mesopotamia), in Iraq (Mesopotamia), Africa, and the Persian Gulf. Though some Christians see the garden as metaphorical, symbolizing God's love and favor.

The origin of the term "Eden", which in Hebrew means "delight", may lie with the word edinu, which itself derives from the Sumerian term EDIN. The Sumerian term means steppe, plain, desert or wilderness, so the connection between the words may be coincidental. This word is known to have been used by the Sumerians to refer to the arid lands west of the Euphrates. Alan Millard has put forward a case for the name deriving from the Semitic stem dn, meaning "abundant, lush".

【詞彙】

genesis n. 起源

myth n. 神話，神話式的人物（或事物），虛構的故事，荒誕的說法

theodicy n. 〔宗〕（基督教）自然神學，神義論，神正論

controversy n. 爭論，辯論，論戰

hypotheses n. 臆測，假定

metaphorical adj. 隱喻性的，比喻性的

Hebrew n. 希伯來人，希伯來語

coincidental adj. 一致的，符合的，巧合的

arid　　　　adj.　　乾旱的，貧瘠的（土地等），無趣的，沉悶的

Euphrates　　　　n.　　幼發拉底河

abundant　　　　adj.　　豐富的，充裕的，豐富，盛產，富於

lush　　　　adj.　　青蔥的，味美的，豪華的，繁榮的

Tigris　　　　n.　　底格里斯河（位於西南亞，流經土耳其和伊拉克）

【問題】

1.What are the four rivers in Eden?

2.What does the origin of the term 「Eden」 mean in Hebrew?

第二節 相關知識連結

一、諾亞方舟

【中文簡介】

諾亞方舟是出自聖經《創世紀》中的一個引人入勝的傳說。由於偷吃禁果，亞當、夏娃被逐出伊甸園。亞當活了930歲，他和夏娃的子女無數，他們的後代子孫越來越多，逐漸遍布整個大地。此後，該隱誅弟，揭開了人類互相殘殺的序幕。人類打著原罪的烙印，上帝詛咒了土地，人們不得不付出艱辛的勞動才能果腹，因此怨恨與惡念日增。人們無休止地相互厮殺、爭鬥、掠奪，人世間的暴力和罪惡簡直到了無以復加的地步。

上帝看到了這一切，他非常後悔造了人，對人類犯下的罪孽感到十分憂傷。上帝說：「我要將所造的人和走獸並昆蟲以及空中的飛鳥都從地上消滅。」但是他又捨不得把他的造物全部毀掉，他希望新一代的人和動物能夠比較聽話，悔過自新，建立一個理想的世界。

在罪孽深重的人群中，只有諾亞在上帝眼前蒙恩。上帝認為他是一個義人，很守本分；他的三個兒子在父親的嚴格教育下也沒有誤入歧途。諾亞也常告誡周圍的人們，應該趕快停止作惡，從充滿罪惡的生活中擺脱出來。但人們對他的話都不以為然，繼續我行我素，一味地作惡享樂。

上帝選中了諾亞一家：諾亞夫婦、三個兒子及其媳婦們，作為新一代人類的種子保存下來。上帝告訴他們七天之後就要實施大毀滅，要他們用歌斐木造一艘方舟，一間一間分開造，裡外抹上松香。這艘方舟要長300肘、寬50肘、高30肘。方舟上邊要留有透光的窗戶，旁邊要開一道門。方舟要分上、中、下三層。他們立即照辦。

上帝看到方舟造好了，就說：「看哪，我要使洪水在地上泛濫，毀滅天下，凡地上有血肉、有氣息的活物無一不死。我卻要與你立約，你同你的妻子、兒子、兒媳都要進入方舟。凡潔淨的畜類，你要帶七公七母；不潔淨的畜類，你要帶一公一母；空中的飛鳥也要帶七公七母。這些都可以留種，將來在地上生殖。」

2月17日那天，諾亞600歲生辰，海洋的泉源都裂開了，巨大的水柱從地下噴射而出；天上的窗戶都敞開了，大雨日夜不停，降了整整40　天。水無處可流，迅速上漲，比最高的山巔都要高出15吋。凡是在旱地上靠肺呼吸的動物都死了，只留下方舟裡人和動物安然無恙。方舟載著上帝的厚望漂泊在無邊無際的汪洋上。

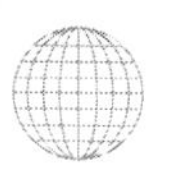

諾亞方舟

上帝顧念諾亞和方舟中的飛禽走獸，便下令止雨興風，風吹著水，水勢漸漸消退。諾亞方舟停靠在亞拉臘山邊。又過了幾十天，諾亞打開方舟的窗戶，放出一隻烏鴉去探聽消息，但烏鴉一去不回。諾亞又把一隻鴿子放出去，要牠去看看地上的水退了沒有。由於遍地是水，鴿子找不到落腳之處，又飛回方舟。七天之後，諾亞又把鴿子放出去，黃昏時分，鴿子飛回來了，嘴裡銜著橄欖葉，很明顯是從樹上啄下來的。又過了七天，諾亞又放出鴿子，這次鴿子不再回來了。諾亞601歲那年的1月1日，地上的水都退乾了。諾亞開門觀望，地上的水退淨了。到2月27日，大地全乾了。於是，上帝對諾亞說：「你和妻兒媳婦可以出舟了。你要把和你同在舟裡的所有飛鳥、動物和一切爬行生物都帶出來，讓牠們在地上繁衍生長吧。」於是，諾亞全家和方舟裡的其他所有生物，都按著種類出來了。後世的人們就用鴿子和橄欖枝來象徵和平。

【英文簡介】

The story of Noah's Ark, according to chapters 6 to 9 in the Book of Genesis, begins with God observing the Earth's corruption and deciding to destroy all life.However, God found one good man, Noah, "a righteous man, blameless among the people of his time", and decided that he would save him. God instructs Noah to make an ark for his family and for representatives of the world's animals and birds in "whose nostrils are the breath of life".

Noah and his family and the animals entered the Ark, and "on the same day all the fountains of the great deep were broken up, and the windows of heaven were opened, and the rain was upon the earth forty days and forty nights". The flood covered even the highest mountains to a depth of more than 6 metres (20 ft), and all creatures died; only Noah and those with him on the Ark were left alive.

At the end of 150 days the Ark came to rest (on the seventeenth day of the seventh month) on the mountains of Ararat. For 150 days again the waters receded, and the hilltops emerged. Noah sent out a raven which "went to and from the Ark until the waters were dried up from the earth". Next, Noah sent a dove out, but it returned having found nowhere to land. After a further seven days, Noah again sent out the dove, and it returned with an olive leaf in its beak, and he knew that the waters had subsided. Noah waited seven days more and sent out the dove once more, and this time it did not return. Then he and his family and all the animals left the Ark, and Noah made a sacrifice to God, and God resolved that he would never again curse the ground because of man, nor destroy all life on it in this manner. Man in turn was instructed never to eat any animal which had not been drained of its blood.

In order to remember this promise, God put a rainbow in the clouds, saying, "Whenever I bring clouds over the earth and the rainbow appears in the clouds, I will see it and remember the everlasting covenant between God and all living creatures of every kind on the earth."

【詞彙】

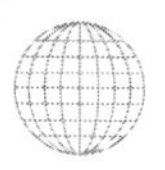

corruption n. 腐敗，貪汙，墮落

righteous adj. 正直的，正當的，正義的

Ark n. 〈聖經〉方舟

recede v. 後退

raven n. 大烏鴉

dove n. 鴿子

sacrifice n. 犧牲，獻身，祭品，供奉 v.犧牲，獻出，獻祭，供奉

drain vt. 排出溝外，喝乾，耗盡 vi.排水，流乾

covenant n. 契約，盟約

subside v. 下沉，沉澱，平息，減退，衰減

【問題】

1.Why did God decide to destroy all the life on Earth?

2.Did Noah make the ark by himself?

二、潘多拉的盒子

【中文簡介】

潘多拉（Pandora）魔盒，又稱潘多拉盒子，潘朵拉的盒子，潘多拉匣子，是一則古希臘經典神話。

潘多拉是宙斯（Zeus）創造的第一個人類女人，主要是要報復人類。因為眾神中的普羅米修斯過分關心人類，於是惹惱了宙斯。宙斯首先命令火神黑菲斯塔斯（Hephaestus）用水土合成攪混，依女神的形象做出一個可愛的女人；再命令愛與美女神阿芙羅黛堤（Aphrodite）給她淋上令男人瘋狂的激素；女神雅典娜（Athena）教女人織布，製造出五顏六色的美麗衣裳，使女人看起來更加鮮艷迷人；完成所有準備工作後，宙斯派遣使神漢密斯（Hermes）說：「放入你狡詐、欺騙、耍賴、偷竊的個性吧！」一個完完全全的女人終於完成了。眾神替她穿上衣服，頭戴兔帽，項配珠鏈，嬌美如新娘。漢密斯出主意說：「叫這個女人潘多拉吧，是諸神送給人類的禮物。」眾神都贊同他的提議。古希臘語中，潘是所有的意思，多拉則是禮物。

宙斯在爭奪神界時，就是得到普羅米修斯及其弟伊皮米修斯的幫助，才登上寶座的。普羅米修斯的名字是「深謀遠慮」的意思。而其弟伊皮米修斯的意思是「後悔」，所以兩兄弟的作風就跟其名字一樣，有著「深謀遠慮」及「後悔」的特性。潘多拉被創造之後，在宙斯的安排下，被送給了伊皮米修斯。因為他知道普羅米修斯不會接受他送的禮物，所以一開始就送給了伊皮米修斯。而伊皮米修斯接受了她，在舉行婚禮時，宙斯命令眾神各將一份禮物放在一個盒子裡，送給潘多拉。而眾神的禮物是好是壞就不得而知了。

普羅米修斯早就警告過伊皮米修斯，千萬不要接受宙斯的禮物，尤其是女人，因為女人是危險的動物。伊皮米修斯就跟其名字一般，娶了潘多拉之後沒多久，就開始後悔了。潘多拉為伊皮米修斯生了7個兒子，但是潘多拉把兒子生下來後，宙斯便把7個兒子用一個盒子封起來，盒子的名字就叫「潘多拉之盒」。潘多拉對此非常憤怒，於是便偷偷地把盒子打開想看看自己的兒子。哪知道一打開，他的前六個兒子便飛了出去，他們的名字叫饑餓、疾病、戰爭、貪婪、氣憤、忌妒和痛苦。從此人間多災多難，但是潘多拉的第七個兒子叫希望。雖然人們受到饑餓、疾病、戰爭、貪婪、氣憤、忌妒和痛苦的困擾，但是人們沒有退縮，因為他們還有希望！

【英文簡介】

The gift of fire had been given to man, but Zeus, King of the gods, was not content that man should possess this treasure in peace. He therefore talked it over with the other gods and together they made for man a woman.

All the gods gave gifts to this new creation. She was named Pandora which means All-gifted, since each of the gods had given her something. The last gift was

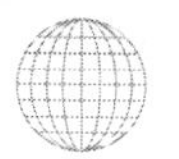

a box in which there was supposed to be a great treasure, but which Pandora was instructed never to open.Then Hermes, the Messenger, took the girl and brought her to a man named Epimetheus.

Epimetheus had been warned to receive no gifts from Zeus, but he was a headless person and Pandora was very lovely. He accepted her. For a while they lived together in happiness.Eventually, however, Pandora's curiosity got the better of her, and she determined to see for herself what treasure it was that the gods had given her. One day when she was alone, she went over to the corner where her box lay and cautiously lifted the lid for a peep. The lid flew up out of her hands and knocked her aside, while before her frightened eyes, dreadful, shadowy shapes flew out of the box in an endless stream.

They were hunger, disease, war, greed, anger, jealousy, toil, and all the griefs and hardships to which man from that day has been subject. At last the stream slackened, and Pandora, who had been paralyzed with fear and horror, found strength to shut her box.

The only thing left in it now, however, was the one good gift the gods had put in among so many evil ones. This was hope, and from that time the hope that is in man's heart is the only thing which has made him able to stand the sorrows that Pandora brought upon him.

【詞彙】

cautiously	adv.	慎重地
slacken	v.	鬆弛，放慢，減弱，減少，減緩
paralyze	vt.	使癱瘓，使麻痹
grief	n.	悲痛，傷心事，不幸，憂傷
peep	n.	窺看，隱約看見

greed n. 貪慾，貪婪

toil n. 辛苦，苦工

【問題】

1.What does the name Pandora mean?

2.How do you understand "Pandora's curiosity got the better of her"?

第三節 練習

1.Match the synonymic phrases.

A.take its/their/a heavy toll on sb/sth a.to declare, to proclaim

B. take over b. used to mention sth that happens immediately afterwards, esp. sth that causes surprise, disappointment, etc.

C.blow itself out (of a storm) c.to lose force or cease entirely

D.only to do sth d.to gain control

E.announce e.to have a bad effect on sb/ sth

F.not that f.although it is not true that

2.Translate the following sentences into English.

（1）她的聲波在清冽的空間擴散，像清甜的冰糖漸漸融化。

（2）葉子出水很高，像婷婷的舞女的裙。

（3）和平萬歲！

（4）打鈴了！

（5）從窗戶裡傳來了音樂聲。

（6）我一生中從未見過這樣的事。

3.Paraphrase. Tell the meanings of the following sentences in your own words.

（1） Not that we didn't have our troubles.

（2） By then the snow had made a blanket of white darkness, but I knew only too well there should have been no creek there.

（3） There was only one thing to do. Camp for the night and hope that by morning the storm would have blown itself out.

（4） The cold and loss of blood were taking their toll.

4.Cloze. Fill in the blanks according to the text: Maheegun My Brother.

That summer Maheegun and I became （1）partners. We hunted the grasshoppers that leaped （2）like little rockets. And in the fall, after snow our （3）took us to the nearest meadows in search of field mice. By then, Maheegun was half （4）. Gone was the puppy-wool coat, in its place was a （5）black （6）.

The winter months that came soon after were the （7）I could remember. They belonged only to Maheegun and （8）. Often we would make a fire in the （9）. Maheegun would lay his head between his front （10）, with his eyes on me as I told him stories.

5.Complete each of the following sentences with the most likely answer.

（1） If you explained the situation to your solicitor, he______able to advise you much better than I can.

A.would be B.will have been

C.was D.were

（2） ______, Mr. Wells is scarcely in sympathy with the working class.

A.Although he is a socialist B.Even if he is a socialist

C.Being a socialist D.Since he is a socialist

(3) His remarks were______annoy everybody at the meeting.

A.so as to B.such as to

C.such to D.as much as to

(4) James has just arrived, but I didn't know he______until yesterday.

A.will come B.was coming

C.had been coming D.came

(5) ______conscious of my moral obligations as a citizen.

A.I was and always will be B.I have to be and always will be

C.I had been and always will be D.I have been and always will be

(6) Because fuel supplies are finite and many people are wasteful, we will have to install______solar heating device in our home.

A.some type of B.some types of a

C.some type of a D.some types of

(7) I went there in 1984, and that was the only occasion when I______the journey in exactly two days.

A.must take B.must have made

C.was able to make D.could make

(8) I know he failed his last test, but really he's______stupid.

A.something but B.anything but

C.nothing but D.not but

(9) Do you know Tim's brother? He is______than Tim.

A.much more sportsman B.more of a sportsman

C.more of sportsman D.more a sportsman

（10） That was not the first time he us.I think it's high time we______strong actions against him.

A.betrayed...take B.had betrayed...took

C.has betrayed...took D.has betrayed...will take

6.Reading comprehension.

One of the good things for men in women's liberation is that men no longer have to pay women the old-fashioned courtesies.

In an article on the new manners, Ms. Holmes says that a perfectly able woman no longer has to act helplessly in public as if she were a model. For example, she doesn't need help getting in and out of cars, "Women get in and out of cars twenty times a day with babies and dogs. Surely they can get out by themselves at night just as easily."

She also says there is no reason for a man to walk on the outside of a woman on the sidewalk. "Historically, the man walked on the inside so he caught the garbage thrown out of a window. Today a man is supposed to walk on the outside. A man should walk where he wants to. So should a woman. If, out of love and respect, he actually wants to take the blows, he should walk on the inside — because that's where attackers are all hiding these days."

As far as manners are concerned, I suppose I have always been a supporter of women's liberation. Over the years, out of a sense of respect, I imagine, I have refused to trouble women with outdated courtesies.

It is usually easier to follow rules of social behavior than to depend on one's own taste. But rules may be safely broken, of course, by those of us with the gift of natural grace. For example, when a man and woman are led to their table in a restaurant and the waiter pulls out a chair, the woman is expected to sit in the chair. That is according to Ms. Ann Clark. I have always done it the other way, according to my wife.

It came up only the other night. I followed the hostess to the table, and when she pulled the chair out I sat on it, quite naturally, since it happened to be the chair I wanted to sit in.

"Well," my wife said, when the hostess had gone, "you did it again."

"Did what?" I asked, utterly confused.

"Took the chair."

Actually, since I'd walked through the restaurant ahead of my wife, it would have been awkward, I should think, not to have taken the chair. I had got there first, after all.

Also, it has always been my custom to get in a car first, and let the woman get in by herself. This is a courtesy I insist on as the stronger sex, out of love and respect. In times like these, there might be attackers hidden about. It would be unsuitable to put a woman in a car and then shut the door on her, leaving her at the mercy of some bad fellow who might be hiding in the back seat.

（1） It can be concluded from the passage that ______.

A.men should walk on the inside of a sidewalk

B.women are becoming more capable than before

C.in women's liberation men are also liberated

D.it's safe to break rules of social behavior

（2） The author was "utterly confused" because he ______.

A.took the chair out of habit　　B.was trying to be polite

C.was slow in understanding D.had forgotten what he did

（3） He "took the chair" for all the following reasons EXCEPT that ______.

A.he got to the chair first B.he happened to like the seat

C.his wife ordered him to do so D.he' d walked ahead of his wife

（4） The author always gets in a car before a woman because he ______.

A.wants to protect her B.doesn't need to help her

C.chooses to be impolite to her D.fears attacks on him

（5） The author is ______about the whole question of manners and women's liberation.

A.joking B.satirical

C.serious D.critical

（6） Which of the following best states the main idea of the passage? ______

A.Manners ought to be thrown away altogether.

B.In manners one should follow his own judgment.

C.Women no longer need to be helped in public.

D.Men are not expected to be courteous to women.

第六章 環保篇

第一節 文化背景知識補充

《寂靜的春天》

【中文簡介】

《寂靜的春天》1962年在美國問世時，是一本很有爭議的書，是一本標誌著人類首次關注環境問題的著作。它那驚世駭俗的關於農藥危害人類環境的預言，不僅受到與之利害攸關的生產與經濟部門的猛烈抨擊，而且也強烈震撼了社會廣大民眾。你若有心去翻閱1960年代以前的報紙或書刊，就會發現幾乎找不到「環境保護」這個詞。這就是說，環境保護在那時並不是一個存在於社會意識和科學討論中的概念。確實，回想一下長期流行於全世界的口號——「向大自然宣戰」、「征服大自然」，在這兒，大自然僅僅是人們征服與控制的對象，而非保護並與之和諧相處的對象。人類的這種意識大概起源於洪荒的原始年月，一直持續到20世紀。沒有人懷疑它的正確性，因為人類文明的許多進展是基於此意識而獲得的，人類當前的許多經濟與社會發展計劃也是基於此意識而制訂的。瑞秋· 卡森（Rachel Carson）第一次對這一人類意識的絕對正確性提出了質疑。這位瘦弱、身患癌症的女學者，是否知道她是在向人類的基本意識和幾千年的社會傳統挑戰？《寂靜的春天》出版兩年之後，她心力交瘁，與世長辭。作為一個學者與作家，卡森所遭受的詆毀和攻擊是空前的，但她所堅持的思想終於為人類環境意識的啟蒙點燃了一盞明亮的燈。

《寂靜的春天》

【作者簡介】

瑞秋· 卡森，1907年5月27日生於賓夕法尼亞州泉溪鎮，並在那兒度過童年。她於1935年至1952年間供職於美國聯邦政府所屬的魚類及野生生物調查所，這使她有機會接觸到許多環境問題。在此期間，她曾寫過一些有關海洋生態的著作，如《在海風下》　、《海的邊緣》和《環繞著我們的海洋》。這些著作使她獲得了一流作家的聲譽。

第二節 相關知識連結

一、可持續發展

【中文簡介】

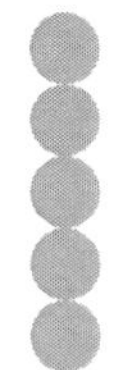

「可持續發展」（sustainable development）的概念最先是在1972 年於斯德哥爾摩舉行的聯合國人類環境研討會上正式提出的。這次研討會雲集了全球工業化和發展中國家的代表，共同界定人類在締造一個健康和富有生機的環境上所享有的權利。自此以後，各國致力界定「可持續發展」的含義，現在擬出的定義已有幾百個之多，涵蓋範圍包括國際、區域、地方及特定界別的層面。最廣泛採納的定義，是在1987年由世界環境及發展委員會所發表的布特蘭報告書中所載的定義，即：既滿足當代人的需求，又不對後代人滿足其需求的能力構成危害的發展稱為可持續發展。它們是一個密不可分的系統，既要達到發展經濟的目的，又要保護好人類賴以生存的大氣、淡水、海洋、土地和森林等自然資源和環境，使子孫後代能夠永續發展和安居樂業。可持續發展與環境保護既有聯繫，又不等同。環境保護是可持續發展的重要方面。可持續發展的核心是發展，但要求在嚴格控制人口、提高人口素質和保護環境、資源永續利用的前提下進行經濟和社會的發展。發展是可持續發展的前提；人是可持續發展的中心；可持續的長久的發展才是真正的發展。

【英文簡介】

Sustainable development is a pattern of resource use that aims to meet human needs while preserving the environment so that these needs can be met not only in the present, but also for future generations. The term was used by the Brundtland Commission which coined what has become the most often-quoted definition of sustainable development as development that "meets the needs of the present without compromising the ability of future generations to meet their own needs."

Sustainable development ties together concern for the carrying capacity of natural systems with the social challenges facing humanity. As early as the 1970s "sustainability" was employed to describe an economy "in equilibrium with basic ecological support systems." Ecologists have pointed to the "limits of growth" and presented the alternative of a "steady state economy" in order to address environmental concerns.

The field of sustainable development can be conceptually broken into three constituent parts: environmental sustainability, economic sustainability and sociopolitical sustainability.

【詞彙】

preserve vt. 保護，保持，保存，保藏 vi.做蜜餞，禁獵 n. 蜜餞，果醬，禁獵地，禁區，防護物

commission n. 委任，委託，代辦（權），代理（權），犯（罪），佣金 vt.委任，任命，委託，委託製作，使服役

ecological adj. 生態學的，社會生態學的

alternative n. 二中擇一，可供選擇的辦法、事物 adj.選擇性的，二中擇一的

sustainable adj. 可以忍受的，足可支撐的，養得起的

constituent n. 選民，成分，構成部分

【問題】

1.How to define sustainable development?

2.What are the three parts that sustainable development can be conceptually divided into?

二、《中國21世紀議程》簡介

【中文簡介】

1992年聯合國環境與發展大會通過了《21世紀議程》，中國政府做出了履行《21世紀議程》等文件的莊嚴承諾。1994年3月25日，《中國21世紀議程》經中國國務院第十六次常務會議審議通過。《中國21世紀議程》共20章，包括78個方案領域，主要內容分為四大部分：

第一部分，可持續發展總體戰略與政策。論述了提出中國可持續發展戰略的背景和必要性；提出了中國可持續發展的戰略目標、戰略重點和重大行動，可持續發展的立法和實施，制定促進可持續發展的經濟政策，參與國際環境與發展領域合作的原則立場和主要行動領域。

第二部分，社會可持續發展。包括人口、居民消費與社會服務，消除貧困，衛生與健康、人類住區和防災減災等。其中最重要的是實行計劃生育、控制人口數量和提高人口素質。

第三部分，經濟可持續發展。《議程》把促進經濟快速增長作為消除貧困、提高人民生活水準、增強綜合國力的必要條件。

第四部分，資源的合理利用與環境保護。包括水、土等自然資源保護與可持續利用。還包括生物多樣性保護，防治土地荒漠化，防災減災等。

第三節 練習

1.Translate the following phrases.

（1）賞心悅目

（2）致命的武器

（3）侵犯某人的隱私

（4）農業的精耕細作

（5）緩和口氣

（6）自然保護區

（7）空氣汙染

（8）外來的物種

（9）創造奇蹟

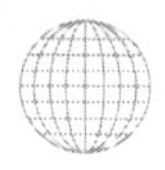

（10）克制衝動

2.Translate the following sentences into English.

（1）秋天，通過松林的屏風，橡樹、楓樹和白樺樹閃射出火焰般的彩色光輝。

（2）曾經一度是那麼吸引人的小路旁，現在排列著彷彿火災劫後焦黃、枯萎的植物。

（3）不是魔法，也不是敵人的行動使這個受災世界的生命無法復生，而是人們自己使自己受害。

（4）是什麼東西使得美國無數城鎮的春天之音沉寂下來了呢？這本書試探著給予解答。

（5）我的論點不是堅絕不用化學殺蟲劑。我要強調的是，我們把有毒的化學製品和對生物有效的化學製品不加區分地交到人們手中，而這些人在很大程度上或者完全不知道這些化學藥品的潛在危害。

3.Paraphrase. Tell the meanings of the following sentences in your own words.

（1） Then some evil spell settled on the community: mysterious diseases swept the flocks of chickens; the cattle and sheep sickened and died.

（2） To a large extent, the physical form and the habits of the earth's vegetation and its animal life have been molded by the environment.

（3） The rapidity of change follows the impetuous pace of man rather than the deliberate pace of nature.

（4） The whole process of spraying seems caught up in an endless spiral.

（5） We have subjected enormous numbers of people to contact with these poisons, without their consent and often without their knowledge.

4.Cloze. Fill in the blanks according to the text: Silent Spring

It is not my (1) that chemical insecticides must never be used. I do (2) that we have put poisonous and biologically (3) chemicals indiscriminately into the hands of persons largely or wholly (4) of their (5) for harm. We have subjected enormous numbers of people to (6) with these poisons, without their (7) and often without their knowledge. I contend, furthermore, that we have allowed these chemicals to be used with little or no advance (8) of their effect on soil, water, (9), and man himself. Future generations are unlikely to forgive our lack of (10) for the integrity of the natural world that supports all life.

5.Complete each of the following sentences with the most likely answer.

(1) I was to have made a speech if ______.

A.I was not called away　　B.nobody would have called me away

C.I had not been called away　　D.nobody called me away

(2) I felt that I was not yet______to travel abroad.

A.too strong　　B.strong enough

C.so strong　　D.enough strong

(3) The plane found the spot and hovered close enough to______that it was a car.

A.ensure　　B.examine

C.verify　　D.testify

(4) The encouraging factor is that the______majority of people find the idea of change acceptable.

A.numerous　　B.vast

C.most　　D.massive

(5) The increase in student numbers______many problems for the

universities.

A.forces B.presses

C.provides D.poses

（6） Please______from smoking until the aero plane is airborne.

A.refrain B.prevent

C.resist D.restrain

（7） Reporters and photographers alike took great______at the rude way the actor behaved during the interview.

A.annoyance B.offence

C.resentment D.irritation

（8） Topics for composition should be______to the experiences and interests of the students.

A.concerned B.dependent

C.connecting D.relevant

（9） The novel contains some marvelously revealing______of rural life in the 19th century.

A.glances B.glimpses

C.glares D.gleams

（10） Sometimes the student may be asked to write about his______on a certain book or article that has some bearing on the subject being studied.

A.reaction B.comment

C.impression D.comprehension

6.Reading comprehension.

The destruction of our natural resources and contamination of our food supply continue to occur, largely because of the extreme difficulty in affixing legal responsibility on those who continue to treat our environment with reckless abandon. Attempts to prevent pollution legislation, economic incentives and friendly persuasion have been met by lawsuits, personal and industrial denial and long delays — not only in accepting responsibility, but more importantly, in doing something about it.

It seems that only when government decides it can afford tax incentives or production sacrifices is there any initiative for change. Where is industry's and our recognition that protecting mankind's great treasure is the single most important responsibility? If ever there will be time for environmental health professionals to come to the frontlines and provide leadership to solve environmental problems, that time is now.

We are being asked, and, in fact, the public is demanding that we take positive action.It is our responsibility as professionals in environmental health to make the difference. Yes, the ecologists, the environmental activists and the conservationists serve to communicate, stimulate thinking and promote behavioral change. However, it is those of us who are paid to make the decisions to develop, improve and enforce environmental standards, I submit, who must lead the charge.

We must recognize that environmental health issues do not stop at city limits, county lines, state or even federal boundaries. We can no longer afford to be tunnelvisioned in our approach. We must visualize issues from every perspective make the objective decisions. We must express our views clearly to prevent media distortion and public confusion.I believe we have a three-part mission for the present. First, we must continue to press for improvements in the quality of life that people can make for themselves. Second, we must investigate and understand the link between environment and health. Third, we must be able to communicate technical information in a form that citizens can understand. If we can accomplish these three goals in this decade, maybe we can finally stop environmental degradation, and not merely hold it back. We will then be able to spend pollution dollars truly on prevention rather than on bandages.

（1） We can infer from the first two paragraphs that the industrialists disregard environmental protection chiefly because ______.

A） they are unaware of the consequences of what they are doing

B） they are reluctant to sacrifice their own economic interests

C） time has not yet come for them to put due emphasis on it

D） it is difficult for them to take effective measures

（2） The main task now facing ecologists, environmental activists and conservationists is______

A） to prevent pollution by legislation, economic incentives and persuasion

B） to arouse public awareness of the importance of environmental protection

C） to take radical measures to control environmental pollution

D） to improve the quality of life by enforcing environmental standards

（3） The word tunnel-visioned （Line 2, Para. 4） most probably means ______.

A） narrow-minded

B） blind to the facts

C） short-sighted

D） able to see only one aspect

（4） Which of the following, according to the author, should play the leading role in the solution of environmental problems? ______

A) Legislation and government intervention.

B) The industry's understanding and support.

C) The efforts of environmental health professionals.

D) The cooperation of ecologists, environmental activists and conservationists.

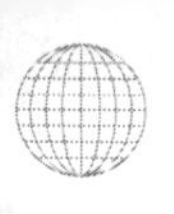

第七章 文學篇

第一節 文化背景知識補充

一、莎士比亞

【中文簡介】

莎士比亞（W. William Shakespeare, 1564—1616），英國文藝復興時期偉大的劇作家、詩人，歐洲文藝復興時期人文主義文學的集大成者，於西元1564年4月23日生於英格蘭華威郡亞芬河畔史特拉福。代表作有四大悲劇《哈姆雷特》（Hamlet）、《奧賽羅》（Othello）、《李爾王》（King Lear）和《馬克白》（Macbeth），四大喜劇《第十二夜》、《仲夏夜之夢》、《威尼斯商人》和《無事生非》（《皆大歡喜》），歷史劇《亨利四世》、《亨利六世》和《理查二世》等。還寫過154首十四行詩，三或四首長詩。他是「英國戲劇之父」，本· 瓊斯稱他為「時代的靈魂」，馬克思稱他為「人類最偉大的天才之一」。他還被稱為「人類文學奧林匹斯山上的宙斯」。雖然莎士比亞只用英文寫作，但他卻是世界著名作家。他的大部分作品都被譯成多種文字，其劇作也在許多國家上演。

一般來說，莎士比亞的戲劇創作可分為以下三個時期：

第一時期（1590—1600），以寫作歷史劇、喜劇為主，有9 部歷史劇、10部喜劇和2部悲劇。9部歷史劇中除《約翰王》寫的是13 世紀初的英國歷史外，其他8部是內容相銜接的兩個4 部曲：《亨利六世》上、中、下篇與《查理三世》，《查理二世》、《亨利四世》（被稱為最成功的歷史劇）上、下篇與《亨利五世》。這些歷史劇概括了英國歷史上百餘年間的動亂，塑造了一系列正、反面君主的形象，反映了莎士比亞反對封建割據，擁護中央集權，譴責暴君暴政，要求開明君主進行自上而下改革，建立和諧社會關係的人文主義政治與道德理想。

第二時期（1601—1607），以悲劇為主，寫了3 部羅馬劇、 5 部悲劇和3部「陰暗的喜劇」或「問題劇」。四大悲劇《哈姆雷特》 、《奧賽羅》 、《李爾王》 、《馬克白》和悲劇《雅典的泰門》標誌著作者對時代、人生的深入思考，著力塑造了這樣一些新時代的悲劇主人翁：他們從中世紀的禁錮和矇昧中醒來，在近代黎明照耀下，雄心勃勃地想要發展或完善自己，但又不能克服時代和自身的侷限，終於在與環境和內心敵對勢力的力量懸殊鬥爭中，遭到不可避免的失敗和犧牲。

第三時期（1608—1613），傾向於妥協和幻想的悲喜劇或傳奇劇。主要作品是4部悲喜劇或傳奇劇《泰爾親王里克里斯》 、《辛白林》 、《冬天的故事》 、《暴風雨》。這些作品多寫失散、團聚、誣陷、昭雪等內容。儘管仍然堅持人文主義理想，對黑暗現實有所揭露，但矛盾的解決主要靠魔法、幻想、機緣巧合和偶然事件，並以宣揚寬恕、容忍、妥協、和解告終。

【英文簡介】

William Shakespeare (26 April, 1564 — 23 April, 1616) was an English poet and playwright, widely regarded as the greatest writer in the English language and the world's preeminent dramatist. He is often called England's national poet and the "Bard of Avon" (or simply "The Bard"). His surviving works consist of 38 plays, 154 sonnets, two long narrative poems, and several other poems. His plays have been translated into every major living language, and are performed more often than those of any other playwright.

Shakespeare produced most of his known work between 1590 and 1613. His early plays were mainly comedies and histories, genres he raised to the peak of sophistication and artistry by the end of the sixteenth century. He then wrote mainly tragedies until about 1608, including Hamlet, King Lear, and Macbeth, considered

some of the finest examples in the English language. In his last phase, he wrote tragicomedies, also known as romances, and collaborated with other playwrights. Many of his plays were published in editions of varying quality and accuracy during his lifetime. In 1623, two of his former theatrical colleagues published the First Folio, a collected edition of his dramatic works that included all but two of the plays now recognized as Shakespeare's.

Shakespeare was a respected poet and playwright in his own day, but his reputation did not rise to its present heights until the nineteenth century. The Romantics, in particular, acclaimed Shakespeare's genius, and the Victorians hero-worshipped Shakespeare with a reverence that George Bernard Shaw called "bardolatry". In the twentieth century, his work was repeatedly adopted and rediscovered by new movements in scholarship and performance. His plays remain highly popular today and are constantly performed and reinterpreted in diverse cultural and political contexts throughout the world.

Plays

Scholars have often noted four periods in Shakespeare's writing career — until the mid-1590s, he wrote mainly comedies influenced by Roman and Italian models and history plays in the popular chronicle tradition. His second period began in about 1595 with the tragedy Romeo and Juliet and ended with the tragedy of Julius Caesar in 1599. During this time, he wrote what are considered his greatest comedies and histories. From about 1600 to about 1608, his "tragic period", Shakespeare wrote mostly tragedies, and from about 1608 to 1613, mainly tragicomedies, also called romances.

The first recorded works of Shakespeare are Richard III and the three parts of Henry VI, written in the early 1590s during a vogue for historical drama. Shakespeare's plays are difficult to date, however, and studies of the texts suggest that Titus Andronicus, The Comedy of Errors, The Taming of the Shrew and Two

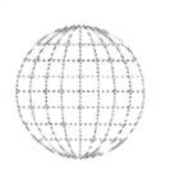

Gentlemen of Verona may also belong to Shakespeare's earliest period.

羅密歐與茱麗葉

Shakespeare's early classical and Italianate comedies, containing tight double plots and precise comic sequences, give way in the mid-1590s to the romantic atmosphere of his greatest comedies. A Midsummer Night's Dream is a witty mixture of romance, fairy magic and comic lowlife scenes. Shakespeare's next comedy, the equally romantic The Merchant of Venice, contains a portrayal of the vengeful Jewish moneylender Shylock which reflected Elizabethan views but may appear prejudiced to modern audiences. The wit and wordplay of Much Ado about Nothing, the charming rural setting of As You Like It, and the lively merrymaking of Twelfth Night complete Shakespeare's sequence of great comedies. After the lyrical Richard Ⅱ, written almost entirely in verse, Shakespeare introduced prose comedy into the histories of the late 1590s, Henry Ⅳ, parts 1 and 2, and Henry Ⅴ. His characters become more complex and tender as he switches deftly between comic and serious scenes, prose and poetry, and achieves the narrative variety of his mature work. This period begins and ends with two tragedies: Romeo and Juliet, the famous romantic tragedy of sexually charged adolescence, love, and death; and Julius Caesar — based on Sir Thomas North's 1579 translation of Plutarch's Parallel Lives — which introduced a new kind of drama. According to Shakespearean scholar James Shapiro, in Julius Caesar "the various strands of politics, character, inwardness, contemporary events, even Shakespeare's own reflections on the act of writing, began to infuse each other".

《哈姆雷特》

Shakespeare's so-called "tragic period" lasted from about 1600 to 1608, though he also wrote the so-called "problem plays" Measure for Measure, Troilus and Cressida, and All's Well That Ends Well during this time and had written tragedies before.Many critics believe that Shakespeare's greatest tragedies represent the peak of his art. The hero of the first, Hamlet, has probably been more discussed than any other Shakespearean character, especially for his famous soliloquy "To be or not to be; that is the question." Unlike the introverted Hamlet, whose fatal flaw is hesitation, the heroes of the tragedies that followed, Othello and King Lear, are undone by hasty errors of judgment. The plots of Shakespeare's tragedies often hinge on such fatal errors or flaws, which overturn order and destroy the hero and those he loves. In Othello, the villain Iago stokes Othello's sexual jealousy to the point where he murders the innocent wife who loves him. In King Lear, the old king commits the tragic error of giving up his powers, initiating the events which lead to the murder of his daughter and the torture and blinding of the Earl of Gloucester. According to the critic Frank Kermode, "the play offers neither its good characters nor its audience any relief from its cruelty". In Macbeth, the shortest and most compressed of Shakespeare's tragedies, uncontrollable ambition incites Macbeth and his wife, Lady Macbeth, to murder the rightful king and usurp the throne, until their own guilt destroys them in turn. In this play, Shakespeare adds a supernatural element to the tragic structure. His last major tragedies, Antony and Cleopatra and Coriolanus, contain some of Shakespeare's finest poetry and were considered his most successful tragedies by the poet and critic T. S. Eliot.

【詞彙】

baptize	v.	施行洗禮
playwright	n.	劇作家
preeminent	adj.	卓越的
bard	n.	吟遊詩人
sonnet	n.	十四行詩
Stratford	n.	史特拉福
speculation	v.	猜測
artistry	n.	藝術的性質
tragicomedies	n.	悲喜劇
reverence	n.	尊敬，威望

vengeful	adj.	復仇的
prose	n.	散文
inwardness	n.	內在的心性
soliloquy	n.	獨白，自言自語
hinge (on)	v.	隨……而定
fatal	adj.	致命的

【問題】

1.How many plays and sonnets did Shakespeare write?

2.List four comedies in Shakespeare's work.

3.List four tragedies in Shakespeare's work.

莎士比亞名言

1.Frailty, thy name is woman!

女人啊，妳的名字是弱者！

2.To be or not to be, that's a question.

生存還是毀滅，那是個值得思考的問題。

3.Better a witty fool than a foolish wit.

寧為聰明的愚夫，不做愚蠢的才子。

4.A light heart lives long.

豁達者長壽。

5.Do not, for one repulse, give up the purpose that you resolved to effect.

不要只因一次失敗，就放棄你原來決心想達到的目的。

6.In delay there lies no plenty, then come kiss me, sweet and twenty, Youth's a stuff that will not endure.

遷延蹉跎，來日無多，二十麗姝，請來吻我，衰草枯楊，青春易過。

7.The time of life is short; to spend that shortness basely, it would be too long.

人生苦短，若虛度年華，則短暫的人生就太長了。

8.Don't gild the lily.

不要給百合花鍍金／畫蛇添足。

9.The empty vessels make the greatest sound.

滿瓶不響，半瓶 當。

10.The course of true love never did run smooth.

真誠的愛情之路永不會是平坦的。

11.Love, and the same charcoal, burning, needs to find ways to ask cooling. Allow an arbitrary, it is necessary to heart charred.

愛，和炭相同，燒起來，得想辦法叫它冷卻。讓它任意燃燒，那就要把一顆心燒焦。

12.Laughter is the root of all evil.

嘲笑是一切罪惡的根源。

13.Love is like a game of tug-of-war competition not stop to the beginning.

愛就像一場拔河比賽，一開始就不能停下來。

14.I would like now to seriously indifferent room of wonderful.

我只想現在認真過得精彩，無所謂好與壞。

15.Love to talk about a bit of a surprise to people to learn the total patient injury.

談一場戀愛學會了忍耐，總有些意外，會讓人受傷害。

16.If you understand the value of love and love you have given me I have to wait for the future.

只要你明白，珍惜愛與被愛，我願意等待，你給我的未來。

17.Sweet love you, precious, I disdained the situation with regard emperors swap.

你甜蜜的愛，就是珍寶，我不屑把處境跟帝王對調。

18.No matter how long night, the arrival of daylight Association.

黑夜無論怎樣悠長，白晝總會到來。

19.Words can not express true love, loyalty behavior is the best explanation.

真正的愛情是不能用言語表達的，行為才是忠心的最好說明。

20.Love is a woman with the ears, and if the men will love, but love is to use your eyes.

女人是用耳朵戀愛的，而男人如果會產生愛情的話，卻是用眼睛來戀愛。

二、但丁

【中文簡介】

但丁· 阿利吉耶里（Dante Alighieri, 1265—1321），義大利詩人，被恩格斯譽為「中世紀的最後一位詩人，同時又是新時代的最初一位詩人」。現代義大利語的奠基者，歐洲文藝復興時代的開拓人物之一，以長詩《神曲》留名後世。恩格斯評價說：封建的中世紀的終結和現代資本主義紀元的開端，是以一位大人物為標誌的，這位大人物就是義大利人但丁，他是「中世紀的最後一位詩人，同時又是新時代的最初一位詩人」。

但丁於1265 年出生在義大利的佛羅倫斯一個沒落的貴族家庭，出生日期不

詳。但丁一生著作甚豐，其中最有價值的無疑是《神曲》。這部作品透過作者與地獄、煉獄及天國中各種著名人物的對話，反映出中古文化領域的成就和一些重大問題，帶有「百科全書」性質，從中也可隱約窺見文藝復興時期人文主義思想的曙光。在這部長達一萬四千餘行的史詩中，但丁堅決反對中世紀的矇昧主義，表達了執著地追求真理的思想，對歐洲後世的詩歌創作有極其深遠的影響。

但丁

除《神曲》外，但丁還寫了《新生》、《論俗語》、《飨宴》及《詩集》等著作。《新生》中包括三十一首抒情詩，主要抒發對貝亞特麗契的眷戀之情，質樸清麗，優美動人，在「溫柔的新體」這一詩派的詩歌中，它達到了最高的成就。

【英文簡介】

Dante Alighieri (1265 - 1321), was a Florentine poet of the Middle Ages. His central work, the Divina Commedia (originally called "Commedia" and later called "Divina" (divine) by Boccaccio, hence "Divina Commedia"), is often considered the greatest literary work composed in the Italian language and a masterpiece of world literature.

In Italian he is known as "the Supreme Poet". Dante, Petrarch and Boccaccio are also known as "the three fountains" or "the three crowns". Dante is also called the "Father of the Italian language".

Works

The Divine Comedy describes Dante's journey through Hell (Inferno), Purgatory (Purgatorio), and Paradise (Paradiso), guided first by the Roman poet Virgil and then by Beatrice, the subject of his love and of another of his works, La Vita Nuova.While the vision of Hell, the Inferno, is vivid for modern readers, the theological niceties presented in the other books require a certain amount of patience and knowledge to appreciate. Purgatorio, the most lyrical and human of the three, also has the most poets in it; Paradiso, the most heavily theological, has the most beautiful and ecstatic mystic passages in which Dante tries to describe what he confesses he is unable to convey (e.g., when Dante looks into the face of God: "all'alba fantasia qui manc possa" — "at this high moment, ability failed my capacity to describe," Paradiso, ⅩⅩⅫ, 142).

Dante wrote the Comedy in a new language he called "Italian", based on the regional dialect of Tuscany, with some elements of Latin and of the other regional dialects. By creating a poem of epic structure and philosophic purpose, he established that the Italian language was suitable for the highest sort of expression.In French, Italian is nicknamed la langue de Dante. Publishing in the vernacular language marked Dante as one of the first (among others such as Geoffrey

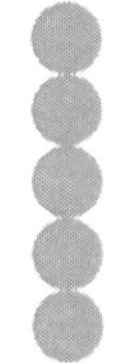

Chaucer and Giovanni Boccaccio) to break from standards of publishing in only Latin (the languages of liturgy, history, and scholarship in general). This break allowed more literature to be published for a wider audience — setting the stage for greater levels of literacy in the future.

Readers often cannot understand how such a serious work may be called a "comedy". In Dante's time, all serious scholarly works were written in Latin (a tradition that would persist for several hundred years more, until the waning years of the Enlightenment) and works written in any other language were assumed to be more trivial in nature.Furthermore, the word "comedy", in the classical sense, refers to works which reflect belief in an ordered universe, in which events not only tended towards a happy or "amusing" ending, but an ending influenced by a providential will that orders all things to an ultimate good. By this meaning of the word, the progression of Dante's pilgrimage from Hell to Paradise is the paradigmatic expression of comedy, since the work begins with the pilgrim's moral confusion and ends with the vision of God.

【詞彙】

Florentine adj. 義大利佛羅倫斯的

Petrarch n. 彼特拉克（1304—1374，義大利詩人、學者、歐洲人文主義運動的主要代表）

Boccaccio n. 薄伽丘（1313—1375，文藝復興時期義大利作家，《十日談》的作者）

verse n. 韻文，詩，詩篇

inferno n. 陰間，地獄

purgatory n. 煉獄

ecstatic adj. 狂喜的，入迷的

enlightenment n. 啟迪，教化

providential adj. 幸運的

pilgrimage n. 朝聖

eloquence n. 雄辯，口才

vernacular adj. 本國的

【問題】

1.What was the era like when Dante was born?

2.What is his greatest work?

3.What title did he earn in the Italian literature?

三、喬叟

【中文簡介】

傑弗里· 喬叟（Geoffrey Chaucer，約1343—1400），英國詩人。1400 年喬叟逝世，安葬在倫敦威斯敏特斯教堂的「詩人之角」（Poet's Corner），他也是第一位葬於此地的詩人。喬叟的詩歌創作分為三個時期：①法國影響時期（1359—1372）：主要翻譯並仿效法國詩人的作品，創作了《悼公爵夫人》（The Book of the Duchess），用倫敦方言翻譯了法國中世紀長篇敘事詩《玫瑰傳奇》等。②義大利影響時期（1372—1386）：詩人接觸了資產階級人文主義的進步思想。這一時期的創作如《百鳥會議》、《特羅伊勒斯和克萊西德》（Troilus and Criseyde）、《好女人的故事》，反映了作者面向生活現實的創作態度和人文主義觀點。③成熟時期（1386—1400）：喬叟在這最後15年裡創作了《坎特伯雷故事集》。無論在內容還是技巧上都達到他創作的頂峰。

喬叟真實地反映了不同社會階層的生活，開創了英國文學的現實主義傳統，對莎士比亞和狄更斯產生了影響。《坎特伯雷故事集》描寫了一群朝聖者（pilgrim）聚集在倫敦一家小旅店裡，準備去坎特伯雷城朝聖。店主人建議朝聖

者們在往返途中各講兩個故事，看誰講得最好。故事集包括了23個故事，其中最精彩的故事有：騎士講的愛情悲劇故事、巴斯婦講的騎士的故事、賣贖罪券者講的勸世寓言故事、教士講的動物寓言故事、商人講的家庭糾紛的故事、農民講的感人的愛情和慷慨義氣行為的故事。

作品廣泛地反映了資本主義萌芽時期英國的社會生活，揭露了教會的腐敗、教士的貪婪和偽善，譴責了扼殺人性的禁慾主義，肯定了世俗的愛情生活。《坎特伯雷故事集》的藝術成就很高，遠遠超過了以前同時代的英國文學作品，是英國文學史上現實主義的第一部典範。作品將幽默和諷刺結合，喜劇色彩濃厚，其中大多數故事用雙韻詩體寫成，對後來的英國文學產生了影響。人物形象鮮明，語言生動活潑。喬叟用富有生命力的倫敦方言進行創作，也為英國文學語言奠定了基礎。他首創的英雄雙韻體為以後的英國詩人所廣泛採用，因而喬叟被譽為「英國詩歌之父」。

【英文簡介】

Geoffrey Chaucer (1343-1400) was an English author, poet, philosopher, bureaucrat, courtier and diplomat. Although he wrote many works, he is best remembered for his unfinished frame narrative The Canterbury Tales. Sometimes called the father of English literature, Chaucer is credited by some scholars as the first author to demonstrate the artistic legitimacy of the vernacular English language, rather than French or Latin.

He is believed to have died of unknown causes on 25 October, 1400, but there is no firm evidence for this date, as it comes from the engraving on his tomb, erected more than one hundred years after his death. There is some speculation — most recently in Terry Jones' book Who Murdered Chaucer? A Medieval Mystery — that he was murdered by enemies of Richard II or even on the orders of his successor Henry IV, but the case is entirely circumstantial. Chaucer was buried in Westminster Abbey in London, as was his right owing to his status as a tenant of the Abbey's close. In 1556 his remains were transferred to a more ornate tomb, making Chaucer the first writer interred in the area now known as Poets' Corner.

Chaucer's first major work, The Book of the Duchess, was an elegy for Blanche of Lancaster (who died in 1369). It is possible that this work was commissioned by her husband John of Gaunt, as he granted Chaucer a £ 10 annuity on June 13, 1374. This would seem to place the writing of The Book of the Duchess between the years 1369 and 1374. Two other early works by Chaucer were Anelida and Arcite and The House of Fame. Chaucer wrote many of his major works in a prolific period when he held the job of customs comptroller for London (1374-1386). His Parlement of Foules, The Legend of Good Women and Troilus and Criseyde all date from this time. Also it is believed that he started work on The Canterbury Tales in the early 1380s. Chaucer is best known as the writer of The Canterbury Tales, which is a collection of stories told by fictional pilgrims on the road to the cathedral at Canterbury; these tales would help to shape English literature.

《坎特伯雷故事集》

The Canterbury Tales contrasts with other literature of the period in the naturalism of its narrative, the variety of stories the pilgrims tell and the varied characters who are engaged in the pilgrimage. Many of the stories narrated by the pilgrims seem to fit their individual characters and social standing, although some of the stories seem ill-fitting to their narrators, perhaps as a result of the incomplete state of the work. Chaucer drew on real life for his cast of pilgrims: the innkeeper shares the name of a contemporary keeper of an inn in Southwark, and real-life identities for the Wife of Bath, the Merchant, the Man of Law and the Student have been suggested. The many jobs that Chaucer held in medieval society — page, soldier, messenger, valet, bureaucrat, foreman and administrator — probably exposed him to many of the types of people he depicted in the Tales. He was able to shape their speech and satirize their manners in what was to become popular literature among people of the same types.

Chaucer's works are sometimes grouped into, first a French period, then an Italian period and finally an English period, with Chaucer being influenced by those countries' literatures in turn. Certainly Troilus and Criseyde is a middle period work with its reliance on the forms of Italian poetry, little known in England at the time, but to which Chaucer was probably exposed during his frequent trips abroad on court business. In addition, its use of a classical subject and its elaborate, courtly language sets it apart as one of his most complete and well-formed works. In Troilus and Criseyde Chaucer draws heavily on his source, Boccaccio, and on the late Latin philosopher Boethius. However, it is The Canterbury Tales, wherein he focuses on English subjects, with bawdy jokes and respected figures often being undercut with humor that has cemented his reputation.

Chaucer also translated such important works as Boethius' Consolation of Philosophy and The Romance of the Rose by Guillaume de Lorris (extended by Jean de Meun). However, while many scholars maintain that Chaucer did indeed translate part of the text of The Romance of the Rose as Roman de la Rose, others claim that this has been effectively disproved. Many of his other works were very loose translations of, or simply based on, works from continental Europe. It is in this role that Chaucer receives some of his earliest critical praise. Eustache Deschamps wrote a ballade on the great translator and called himself a "nettle in Chaucer's garden of poetry". In 1385 Thomas Usk made glowing mention of Chaucer, and John Gower, Chaucer's main poetic rival of the time, also praised him. This reference was later edited out of Gower's Confessio Amantis and it has been suggested by some that this was because of ill feeling between them, but it is likely due simply to stylistic concerns.

【詞彙】

bureaucrat	n.	官僚
courtier	n.	朝臣
legitimacy	n.	合法性，正確性
vernacular	adj.	本國的
pilgrim	n.	聖地朝拜者
Westminster Abbey	n.	威斯敏斯特教堂（英國名人墓地）
cathedral	n.	大教堂
cement	v.	黏合

【問題】

1.What is Chaucer's most outstanding work?

2.What is his status in English literature?

3.What are the three periods of Chaucer's work?

第二節 相關知識連結

一、王爾德

【中文簡介】

奧斯卡· 王爾德（Oscar Wilde，1854—1900），英國唯美主義藝術運動的倡導者，著名的作家、詩人、戲劇家、藝術家。

王爾德生於愛爾蘭都柏林的一個家世卓越的家庭。他的父親威廉姆· 王爾德爵士是一位外科醫生，他的母親是一位詩人與作家。

王爾德自都柏林聖三一學院（Trinity College）畢業後，獲得獎學金，於 1874 年進入牛津大學莫德林學院（Magdalen College）學習。在牛津，王爾德受到了沃爾特· 佩特及約翰· 拉斯金的審美觀念影響，並接觸了新黑格爾派哲學、達爾文進化論和拉斐爾前衛派的作品，這為他之後成為唯美主義先鋒作家確立了方向。

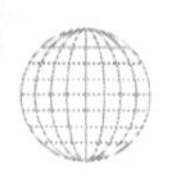

王爾德

代表作品：

小說

《道林· 格雷的畫像》（1891年）

童話集

《快樂王子和其他故事》（1888年）

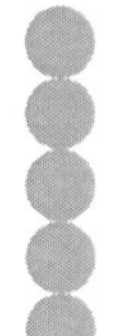

收錄童話

《快樂王子》

《夜鶯與薔薇》

《自私的巨人》

《忠實的朋友》

《了不起的火箭》

《石榴屋》

《少年國王》

《西班牙公主的生日》

《漁人和他的靈魂》

《星孩》

詩作

《詩集》（1881年）

《斯芬克斯》（1894年）

《瑞丁監獄之歌》（1898年）

【英文簡介】

Oscar Fingal O'Flahertie Wills Wilde (1854-1900) was an Irish playwright, poet and author of numerous short stories and one novel. Known for his biting wit, he became one of the most successful playwrights of the late Victorian era in London, and one of the greatest celebrities of his day. Several of his plays continue to be widely performed, especially The Importance of Being Earnest. As the result of a widely covered series of trials, Wilde suffered a dramatic downfall and was imprisoned for two years' hard labour after being convicted of "gross indecency" with other men. After Wilde was released from prison he set sail for Dieppe by the night ferry. He never returned to Ireland or Britain.

Novels:

The Picture of Dorian Gray

Fairy Tales:

The Happy Prince

The Nightingale and the Rose

The Selfish Giant

The Devoted Friend

The Remarkable Rocket

A House of Pomegranates

The Young King

The Birthday of the Infanta

The Fisherman and His Soul

The Star-Child

Poems:

Poems

Sphinx

The Ballad of Reading Gaol

【詞彙】

ballad	n.	民歌，歌謠
downfall	n.	衰敗，垮臺
Dorian	n.	多利安人
earnest	adj.	認真的
ferry	n.	渡船
sphinx	n.	（希臘神話）斯芬克斯

playwright n. 劇作家

【問題】

1.Which play of his continues to be widely performed?

2.Why was he imprisoned for two years?

二、海明威

【中文簡介】

厄尼斯特· 海明威（Ernest Hemingway，1899—1961），美國小說家。1954年度的諾貝爾文學獎獲得者，「新聞體」小說的創始人。

第一次世界大戰爆發後，海明威懷著要親臨戰場感受戰爭的熱切願望，加入美國紅十字會戰場服務隊，投身義大利戰場。大戰結束後，海明威被義大利政府授予十字軍功獎章、銀質獎章和勇敢獎章，獲得中尉軍銜。伴隨榮譽的是他身上237處的傷痕和趕不走的惡魔般的戰爭記憶。

《太陽照常升起》是海明威的第一部重要小說。小說發表於1926年，寫的是像海明威一樣流落在法國的一群美國年輕人。他們在第一次世界大戰後，迷失了前進的方向，戰爭給他們造成了生理上和心理上的巨大傷害，他們非常空虛、苦惱和憂鬱。他們想有所作為，但戰爭使他們精神迷惘，爾虞我詐的社會又使他們非常反感，他們只能在沉淪中度日，美國作家葛楚· 史坦由此稱他們為「迷惘的一代」。這部小說是海明威自己生活道路和世界觀的真實寫照。海明威和他所代表的一個文學流派因而也被人稱為「迷惘的一代」。

海明威

1929年，海明威發表了《永別了，武器》，其中的主人翁亨利是個美國青年，他自願來到義大利戰場參戰。在負傷期間，他愛上了英籍女護士凱瑟琳。亨利努力工作，但在一次撤退時竟被誤認為是德國間諜而險些被槍斃。他只好跳河逃跑，並決定脫離戰爭。為擺脫憲兵的追捕，亨利和凱瑟琳逃到了中立國瑞士。在那裡，他們度過了一段幸福而寧靜的生活。但不久，凱瑟琳死於難產，嬰兒也窒息而亡。亨利一個人被孤獨地留在世界上，他悲痛欲絕，欲哭無淚。小說在戰爭的背景下描寫了亨利和凱瑟琳的愛情，深刻地指出了他們的幸福和愛情是被戰爭推向毀滅的深淵的。

1940年，海明威發表了以西班牙內戰為背景的反法西斯主義的長篇小說《喪鐘為誰而鳴》。作品的主人翁是美國青年喬頓，他志願參加西班牙人民的反法西斯鬥爭，奉命在一支山區游擊隊的配合下，在指定時間炸毀一座具有戰略意義的橋梁。喬頓炸毀了橋梁，在身負重傷的情況下獨自狙擊敵人，等待他的是死亡。喬頓有高度的正義感和責任心，他因自己能為反法西斯鬥爭捐軀而感到光榮和自豪。這部作品是海明威中期創作中思想性最強的作品之一，在相當程度上克服和擺脫了孤獨、迷惘與悲泣的情緒，把個人融入社會中，表現出為正義事業而獻身的崇高精神。

1952年，海明威發表了中篇小說《老人與海》。小說中老漁夫桑提亞哥在海上連續84天沒有捕到魚。起初，有一個叫曼諾林的男孩跟他一道出海，可是過了40天還沒有釣到魚，孩子就被父母安排到另一條船上去了，因為他們認為孩子跟著老頭不會交好運。第85天，老頭兒一清早就把船划出很遠，他出乎意料地釣到了一條比船還大的馬林魚。老頭兒和這條魚周旋了兩天，終於叉中了牠。但受傷的魚在海上留下了一道腥蹤，引來無數鯊魚的爭搶。老人奮力與鯊魚搏鬥，但回到海港時，馬林魚只剩下一副巨大的骨架，老人也精疲力竭地一頭栽倒在陸地上。孩子來看老頭兒，他認為桑提亞哥沒有被打敗。那天下午，桑提亞哥在茅棚中睡著了，夢中他見到了獅子。「一個人並不是生來要被打敗的，你盡可以把他消滅掉，可就是打不敗他。」這是桑提亞哥的生活信念，也是《老人與海》中作者要表明的思想。透過桑提亞哥的形象，作者熱情地讚頌了人類面對艱難困苦時所顯示的堅不可摧的精神力量。孩子準備和老人再度出海，他要學會老人的一切「本領」，這象徵著人類這種「打不敗」的精神將代代相傳。

1961年7月2日，蜚聲世界文壇的海明威用自己的獵槍結束了自己的生命。整個世界都為之震驚，人們紛紛嘆息這位巨人的悲劇。美國人民更是悲悼這位美國重要作家的隕落。

海明威最傑出的作品：

1926年《太陽照常升起》

1929年《永別了，武器》

1940年《喪鐘為誰而鳴》

1952年《老人與海》

海明威名言：

一個人並不是生來要被打敗的，你盡可以把他消滅掉，可就是打不敗他。

生活與鬥牛差不多。不是你戰勝牛，就是牛挑死你。

冰山運動之雄偉壯觀，是因為它只有八分之一在水面上。

沒有失敗，只有戰死。

對一個作家最好的訓練是不快樂的童年。

20世紀的喪鐘為人類而鳴！

只向老人低頭。

每個人都不是一座孤島，一個人必須是這世界上最堅固的島嶼，然後才能成為大陸的一部分。

海明威自題的墓誌銘也能表現出他的思想和語言特色：恕我不起來啦！

【英文簡介】

Ernest Miller Hemingway (July 21, 1899-July 2, 1961) was an American writer and journalist. He was part of the 1920s expatriate community in Paris, and one of the veterans of World War I later known as "the Lost Generation". He received the Pulitzer Prize in 1953 and the Nobel Prize in Literature in 1954 for The Old Man and the Sea.

Hemingway's distinctive writing style is characterized by economy and understatement, and had a significant influence on the development of twentieth-century fiction writing. His protagonists are typically stoical men who exhibit an ideal described as "grace under pressure". Many of his works are now considered classics of American literature.

With the publication of The Sun Also Rises (1926), he was recognized as the spokesman of the "lost generation" (so called by Gertrude Stein). The novel concerns a group of psychologically bruised, disillusioned expatriates living in postwar Paris, who take psychic refuge in such immediate physical activities as eating, drinking, traveling, brawling, and lovemaking.

His next important novel, A Farewell to Arms (1929), tells of a tragic wartime love affair between an ambulance driver and an English nurse. From his experience in the Spanish Civil War came Hemingway's great novel, For Whom the Bell Tolls (1940), which, in detailing an incident in the war, argues for human brotherhood. His novella The Old Man and the Sea (1952) celebrates the indomitable courage of an aged Cuban fisherman.

Famous Quotes

Man is not made for defeat, a man can be destroyed but not defeated.

I always try to write on the principal of the iceberg. There is seven eighths of it under water for every part that shows.

The world is a fine place, and worth fighting for.

A man is an isolated island or not.Sometimes, he must turn himself into the most solid kind of isolated islands in this world in order to be a part of the continent.

Pardon me for not getting up.

Major Novels

- (1926) The Torrents of Spring
- (1926) The Sun Also Rises
- (1929) A Farewell to Arms
- (1937) To Have and Have Not
- (1940) For Whom the Bell Tolls
- (1950) Across the River and Into the Trees
- (1952) The Old Man and the Sea

【詞彙】

expatriate vt. 逐出國外，脫離國籍，放逐 vi.移居國外 n.亡命國外者

veteran n. 老兵，老手，富有經驗的人，退伍軍人

distinctive adj. 與眾不同的，有特色的

protagonist n. （戲劇，故事，小說中的）主角，領導者，積極參加者

stoical adj. 堅忍的，不以苦樂為意的

ambulance n. 戰時流動醫院，救護車

refuge n. 庇護，避難，避難所

indomitable adj. 不屈服的，不屈不撓的

【問題】

1.What prizes did he receive in 1953 and 1954 for The Old Man and the Sea?

2.What's Hemingway's distinctive writing style?

3.When was he recognized as the spokesman of the "lost generation"?

4.List his major novels.

第三節 練習

（練習是基於《現代大學英語》第二冊課文 Lesson One: Another School Year — What For?）

1.Match the synonymic phrases.

A.to average out a.to obtain

B.to be exposed to b.to limit one's business to a particular subject

C.to be stuck for c.to come to an ordinary level

D.to have no business doing sth d.approximately

E.to see to it that... e.to make sure that...

F.to be true of f.in reality

G.to specialize in g.to be trying to get or do sth

H.to be out to do h.not to know what to do in a particular situation

I.in literal time. i.to have no right to do sth

J.to preside over j.to be in charge a meeting or an event

K.to reach for k.to be given experience of it, introduced to it

L.more or less l.to apply to

M.in essence m.it is likely

N.to be employed in doing sth n.by nature

O.chances are o.to spend your time doing sth

2.Translate the following sentences into English.

（1）儘管我是新教師，但是我本來可以給這個傢伙講出許多事情。

（2）你主持的家庭中有民主氣息的熏陶嗎？家裡有「書」嗎？有那種懂得藝術欣賞的人看了不會搖頭的畫嗎？孩子們會聽到巴赫的音樂嗎？

（3）如果你急著去賺錢，或是對自己的無知甚為得意，從而把亞里斯多德或喬叟或愛因斯坦的思想——這個提高你的品位修養的禮物拒之門外，那麼你既不是一個發展到成熟階段的人，也不是一個民主社會有用的成員。

（4）因為一本好書必然是一份禮物；它為你呈現你沒時間去親自體驗的生

活，帶你進入一個你在現實生活中沒時間去親自遊覽的世界。

（5）要是一所大學不能使你們學生，無論作為專門人才還是普通人，去接觸那些你們的頭腦應該有的那些大師們的思想，那麼這所大學就沒有真正的辦學宗旨，也就沒有存在的必要了。

3.Paraphrase. Tell the meanings of the following sentences in your own words.

（1） It would certify that he had specialized in pharmacy, but it would further certify that he had been exposed to some of the ideas mankind has generated within his history.

（2） You will see to it that the cyanide stays out of the aspirin, that the bull doesn't jump the fence, or that your client doesn't go to the electric chair as a result of your incompetence.

（3） If you have no time for Shakespeare, for a basic look at philosophy, for the continuity of the fine arts, for that lesson of man's development we call history — then you have no business being in college.

（4） You are on your way to being that new species of mechanized savage, the pushbutton Neanderthal.

（5） Our colleges inevitably graduate a number of such life forms, but it cannot be said that they went to college; rather the college went through them — without making contact.

4.Cloze. Fill in the blanks according to the text: Another School Year — What For？

And as this is true of the （1）of mankind, so it is true of mankind's spiritual resources. Most of these resources, both （2）and spiritual, are （3）in books. Books are man's （4）（5）. When you have read a book, you have added to your human experience. Read Homer and your mind includes a piece of Homer's mind. Through books you can （6）at least （7）of the mind and experience of

（8），（9），（10） — the list is endless.

I speak, I'm sure, for the faculty of the （11） arts college and for the faculties of the （12） schools as well, when I say that a university has no real （13） and no real purpose except as it （14） in putting you in （15），both as （16） and as humans, with those human minds your human mind needs to （17）. The faculty, （18） its very （19），says （20）. We have been （21） by many people, and by many books, in our （22） to make ourselves some sort of （23） of human experience. We are here to make （24） to you, as best as we can, that （25）.

5.Complete each of the following sentences with the most likely answer.

（1） That trumpet player was certainly loud. But I wasn't bothered by his loudness______by his lack of talent.

A.so much as　　B.rather than

C.as　　D.than

（2） ______, I'll marry him all the same.

A.Was he rich or poor　　B.Whether rich or poor

C.Were he rich or poor　　D.Be he rich or poor

（3） The government has promised to do______lies in its power to ease the hardships of the victims in the flood-stricken area.

A.however　　B.whichever

C.whatever　　D.wherever

（4） ______if I had arrived yesterday without letting you know beforehand?

A.Would you be surprised　　B.Were you surprised

C.Had you been surprised　　D.Would you have been surprised

（5） If not______with the respect he feels due to him, Jack gets very ill-tempered and grumbles all the time.

A.being treated B.treated

C.be treated D.having been treated

（6） It is imperative that students______their term papers on time.

A.hand in B.would hand in

C.have to hand in D.handed in

（7） The less the surface of the ground yields to the weight of a fully-loaded truck, ______to the truck.

A.the greater stress is B.greater is the stress

C.the stress is greater D.the greater the stress

（8） The Minister of Finance is believed______of imposing new taxes to raise extra revenue.

A.that he is thinking B.to be thinking

C.that he is to think D.to think

（9） Issues of price, place, promotion, and product are______conventional concerns in planning marketing strategies.

A.these of the most B.most of those

C.among the most D.among the many of

（10） ______both sides accept the agreement______a lasting peace be established in this region.

A.Only if, will B.If only, would

C.Should, will D.Unless, would

6.Reading comprehension.

For several days I saw little of Mr. Rochester. In the morning he seemed much occupied with business, and in the afternoon gentlemen from the neighborhood called and some times stayed to dine with him. When his foot was well enough, he rode out a great deal.

During this time, all my knowledge of him was limited to occasional meetings about the house, when he would sometimes pass me coldly, and sometimes bow and smile. His changes of manner did not offend me, because I saw that I had nothing to do with the cause of them.

One evening, several days later, I was invited to talk to Mr. Rochester after dinner. He was sitting in his armchair, and looked not quite so severe, and much less gloomy. There was a smile on his lips, and his eyes were bright, probably with wine. As I was looking at him, he suddenly turned, and asked me, "Do you think I'm handsome, Miss Eyre?"

The answer somehow slipped from my tongue before I realized it: "No, sir."

"Ah, you really are unusual! You are a quiet, serious little person, but you can be almost rude."

"Sir, I'm sorry. I should have said that beauty doesn't matter, or something like that."

"No, you shouldn't! I see, you criticize my appearance, and then you stab me in the back! You have honesty and feeling. There are not many girls like you. But perhaps I go too fast. Perhaps you have awful faults to counterbalance your few good points."

I thought to myself that he might have too. He seemed to read my mind, and said quickly, "yes, you're right. I have plenty of faults. I went the wrong way when I was twenty-one, and have never found the right path again. I might have been very different. I might have been as good as you, and perhaps wiser. I am not a bad man, take my word for it, but I have done wrong. It wasn't my character, but circumstances which were to blame. Why do I tell you all this? Because you're the sort of person people tell their problems and secrets to, because you're sympathetic and give them hope."

It seemed he had quite a lot to talk to me. He didn't seem to like to finish the talk quickly, as was the case for the first time.

"Don't be afraid of me, Miss Eyre." He continued. "You don't relax or laugh very much; perhaps because of the effect Lowood school has had on you. But in time you will be more natural with me, and laugh, and speak freely. You're like a bird in a cage. When you get out of the cage, you'll fly very high. Good night."

（1） At the beginning miss Eyre's impressions of Mr. Rochester were all except ______.

A.busy

B.sociable

C.friendly

D.changeable

（2） In "...and all my knowledge of him was limited to occasional meetings about the house..." The word about means ______.

A.around

B.on

C.outside

D.concerning

（3） Why did Mr. Rochester say "...and then you stab me in the back!" ? (Para 7) ______.

A.Because Jane had intended to kill him with a knife

B.Because Jane had intended to be less straightforward

C.Because Jane had regretted having talked to him

D.Because Jane had said something else to correct herself

（4） From what Mr.Rochester told Miss Eyre, we can conclude that he wanted to ______.

A.tell her all his troubles

B.tell her his life experience

C.change her opinion of him

D change his circumstances

（5） At the end of the passage, Mr. Rochester sounded ______.

A.rude

B.cold

C.friendly

D.encouraging

第八章 奧運篇

第一節 奧運知識

一、現代奧運之父古柏坦

【中文簡介】

皮耶· 德· 古柏坦被譽為「現代奧林匹克之父」。他的父親是路易十三皇帝加封的男爵，是個頗有名氣的水彩畫家，擁有大量土地和財產，母親是海牙港附近的諾曼底公爵的後裔，是個虔誠的天主教徒。

1863年1月1日，古柏坦出生於巴黎。優越的貴族之家，提供了良好的教育，童年的他在祖父位於諾曼底的城堡中過著田園牧歌般的生活。他聰明過人，喜愛拳擊、划船、擊劍和騎馬等運動。學生時代，他不但是一名體育愛好者，還熱愛歷史，特別是對古希臘的燦爛文化饒有興趣。他鍾情藝術，喜歡繪畫，擅長鋼琴，擁有超凡的藝術家氣質，難以忍受那些陳舊的學校規章。

古柏坦漸漸有了以體育推動教育改革的想法。但是，古柏坦主張的「充分接觸大自然，進行激烈的體育競技」的主張遭遇社會逆風向。1892年11月25日，古柏坦在索邦巴黎神學院舉行的第5屆法國體育協會聯合會年會上，首次提出「恢復奧林匹克運動會」的主張。1894年6月23日，國際奧林匹克委員會成立，由古柏坦起草的第一部《奧林匹克憲章》獲得通過。1896年4月5日，第一屆現代奧運會在雅典開幕。

1937年9月2日，古柏坦因心臟病突發，在日內瓦湖邊的長椅上辭世。根據他的遺願，他的骨灰和心臟於1938年安葬在奧林匹克運動的發祥地奧林匹亞山下。

【英文簡介】

Le Baron Pierre de Coubertin was born on January 1, 1863 in an established aristocratic family in Paris. His father Charles was a baron granted by Louis XIII and an accomplished artist of watercolor painting. His mother was a devout Catholic and also a descendant of an aristocratic family. They owned a lot of land and property.

古柏坦

Born in an aristocratic family, Coubertin received a very good education, and he lived a pastoral life during his childhood in the castle of his grandfather. So smart as he was, Coubertin liked sports such as boxing, rowing, fencing, horse riding, and etc. When he was a student, he was already not only a sports enthusiast, but also a history and art lover. He was particularly interested in the splendid culture of ancient Greece; he liked painting; and he played the piano. All these made him wear a temperament of artist.

However, the old rules and regulations at school were unbearable to Coubertin. And gradually he had the idea of promoting the education reform through sports. Unfortunately, his concept of "full access to nature, and fierce competition in sports" was too innovative for the society to accept. On November 25, 1892, on the fifth annual meeting of the Union des Soci t s Françaises de Sports Athl tiaues (USFSA) held in the University of La Sorbonne, Coubertin raised the matter of "reviving the Olympic Games" for the first time. On June 23, 1894 the International Olympic Committee was established and the first Olympic Charter drafted by Coubertin was passed. And the first modern Olympic Games were opened on April 5, 1896 in Athens.

On September 2, 1937, Pierre de Coubertin was struck by a heart attack and died on a bench near a lake in Geneva. According to his wishes, his ashes and heart were buried in the birthplace of the Olympic movement at the foot of the Olympia Mountain in 1938.

二、《奧林匹克宣言》的誕生

【中文簡介】

115年前，在法國的索邦大學，29　歲的法國男爵古柏坦發表了長篇演講，號召人們「堅持不懈地追求，實現一個以現代生活條件為基礎的偉大而有益的事業」，這一演講被國際奧委會和國際社會公認為現代奧林匹克運動最早、最權威的文獻，即《奧林匹克宣言》。由於他的努力推進，1894年國際奧委會在巴黎成立，1896年首屆奧運會在雅典舉行。

遺憾的是，由於當時所處的戰爭環境，這部珍貴的手稿沒能公諸於世，古柏坦先生悄悄藏起了這份14頁的法文原稿。經過了第一次和第二次世界大戰，有幸聆聽過演講的人們也都早已作古，一百多年來，那份曾經令人振奮和激動的

《宣言》彷彿早已遺失，並漸漸被世人遺忘。

法國外交分析專家達馬侯爵一直堅信《宣言》尚在人間，歷盡曲折在歐美多個國家不斷尋找線索，終於在紀念國際奧委會誕辰百年前夕，於瑞士一家銀行的保險箱中找到了這份具有重大歷史意義的珍貴文獻。人們可以從泛黃而脆弱的手稿中清晰地看到古柏坦115年前的召喚：「復興奧林匹克運動」。

【英文簡介】

On November 25, 1892, in the University of La Sorbonne, the 29-year-old French Baron Coubertin made a long speech, calling on people to conduct "unremitting pursuit to realize a great and significant cause on the basis of modern living conditions". This speech is considered the first and the most authoritative document about the modern Olympic movement by the International Olympic Committee and the international community; it is entitled the "Olympic Declaration". With the efforts made by Coubertin, the International Olympic Committee was established in Paris in 1894, and the first modern Olympic Games were held in Athens in 1896.

Unfortunately, due to the wartime environment, the precious manuscript was not able to be made public to the world. Mr. Coubertin secretly kept the 14-page French manuscript for a long time. When the first and the second World Wars finally ended, people who were lucky to be at the site to listen the exciting "Declaration" were no long living on this world. It seemed that the manuscript must have been lost, and have been forgotten gradually.

The French diplomatic analyst Marquis Ed Damazin believed that the "Declaration" still existed. Following different clues in countries of the Europe and America, and after twists and turns, he finally found it in a safe of a Swiss bank, just before the centennial of the International Olympic Committee. This precious manuscript with great significance has become yellow and delicate, but we can still clearly see the call of Coubertin 155 years ago: "rejuvenation of the Olympic movement."

第二節 練習

Reading comprehension.

A

Reebok executives do not like to hear their stylish athletic shoes called footwear for yuppies. They contend that Reebok shoes appeal to diverse market segments, especially now that the company offers basketball and children's shoes for the under-18 set and walking shoes for older customers not interested in aerobics or running. The executives also point out that through recent acquisitions they have added hiking boots, dress and casual shoes, and high-performance athletic footwear to their product lines, all of which should attract new and varied groups of customers. Still, despite its emphasis on new markets, Reebok plans few changes in the up market retailing network that helped push sales to 1 billion annually, ahead of all other sports shoe marketers. Reebok shoes, which are priced from $27 to $85, will continue to be sold only in better specialty, sporting goods, and department stores, in accordance with the company's view that consumers judge the quality of the brand by the quality of its distribution. In the past few years, the Massachusetts-based company has imposed limits on the number of its distributors (and the number of shoes supplied to stores), partly out of necessity. At times the unexpected demand for Reebok's exceeded supply, and the company could barely keep up with orders from the dealers it already had. These fulfillment problems seem to be under control now, but the company is still selective about its distributors. At present, Reebok shoes are available in about five thousand retail stores in the United States. Reebok has already anticipated that walking shoes will be the next fitness-related craze, replacing aerobics shoes the same way its brightly colored, soft leather exercise footwear replaced conventional running shoes. Through product diversification and careful market research, Reebok hopes to avoid the distribution problems Nike came across several years ago, when Nike misjudged the strength of the aerobics shoe craze and was forced to unload huge inventories of running shoes through discount stores.

（1） One reason why Reebok's managerial personnel don't like their shoes to be called "footwear for yuppies" is that______

A.they believe that their shoes are popular with people of different age groups.

B.new production lines have been added to produce inexpensive shoes.

C."yuppies" usually evokes a negative image.

D.the term makes people think of prohibitive prices.

（2） Reebok's view that "consumers judge the quality of the brand by the quality of its distribution" implies that______

A.the quality of a brand is measured by the service quality of the store selling it.

B.the quality of a product determines the quality of its distributors.

C.the popularity of a brand is determined by the stores that sell it.

D.consumers believe that first-rate products are only sold by high-quality stores.

（3） Reebok once had to limit the number of its distributors because______

A.its supply of products fell short of demand.

B.too many distributors would cut into its profits.

C.the reduction of distributors could increase its share of the market.

D.it wanted to enhance consumer confidence in its products.

（4） Although the Reebok Company has solved the problem of fulfilling its orders, it______

A.does not want to further expand its retailing network.

B.still limits the number of shoes supplied to stores.

C.is still particular about who sells its products.

D.still carefully chooses the manufacturers of its products.

（5） What lesson has Reebok learned from Nike's distribution problems? ______

A.A company should not sell its high quality shoes in discount stores.

B.A company should not limit its distribution network.

C.A company should do follow-up surveys of its products.

D.A company should correctly evaluate the impact of a new craze on the market.

B

Massive changes in all of the world's deeply cherished sporting habits are underway. Whether it's one of London's parks full of people playing softball, and Russians taking up rugby, or the Super bowl rivaling the British Football Cup Final as a televised spectator event in Britain, the patterns of players and spectators are changing beyond recognition. We are witnessing a globalization of our sporting culture.

That annual bicycle race, the Tour de France, much loved by the French is a good case in point. Just a few years back it was a strictly continental affair with France, Belgium and Holland, Spain and Italy taking part. But in recent years it has been dominated by Colombian mountain climbers, and American and Irish riders.

The people who really matter welcome the shift toward globalization. Peugeot, Michelin and Panasonic are multi-national corporations that want worldwide returns for the millions they invest in teams. So it does them literally a world of good to see this unofficial world championship become just that.

This is undoubtedly an economic-based revolution we are witnessing here, one made possible by communications technology, but made to happen because of marketing considerations. Sell the game and you can sell Cola or Budweiser as well. The skilful way in which American football has been sold to Europe is a good example of how all sports will develop. The aim of course is not really to spread the sport for its own sake, but to increase the number of people interested in the major money-making events. The economics of the Super bowl are already astronomical. With seats at US $5, gate receipts alone were a staggering $10,000,000. The most important statistic of the day, however, was the quality of its Distribution, $100,000,000 in TV advertising fees. Imagine how much that becomes when the eyes of the world are watching.

So it came as a terrible shock, but not really as a surprise, to learn that some people are now suggesting that soccer change from being a game of two 45-minute halves, to one of four 25-minute quarters. The idea is unashamedly to capture more advertising revenue, without giving any thought for the integrity of a sport which relies for its essence on the flowing nature of the action.

Moreover, as sports expand into world markets, and as our choice of sports as consumers also grows, we will demand to see they played at a higher and higher level. In boxing we have already seen numerous, dubious world title categories because people will not pay to see anything less than a "World Tide" fight, and this means that the title fights have to be held in different countries around the world!

（1） Globalization of sporting culture means that ______

A.more people are taking up sports.

B.traditional sports are getting popular.

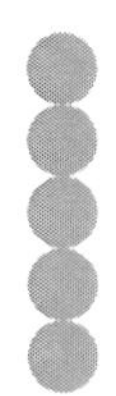

C.many local sports are becoming international.

D.foreigners are more interested in local sports.

（2） Which of the following is NOT related to the massive changes?

A.Good economic returns. B.Revival of sports.

C.Communications technology. D.Marketing strategies.

（3） What is the author's attitude towards the suggestion to change soccer into one of four 25-minute quarters? ______

A.Favorable. B.Unclear. C.Reserved. D.Critical.

（4） People want to see higher-level sports competitions mainly because ______

A.they become more professional than ever.

B.they regard sports as consumer goods.

C.there exist few world-class championships.

D.sports events are exciting and stimulating.

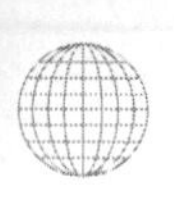

附錄一　歷任美國總統

歷任美國總統簡介

1.喬治·華盛頓（George Washington），1789—1797年，開國總統。

2.約翰·亞當斯（John Adams），聯邦黨，1797—1801年，人稱「老亞當斯」，兒子是第6任美國總統，他們是美國歷史上第一對父子檔總統。

3.湯瑪斯·傑佛遜（Thomas Jefferson），民主共和黨，1801—1809年。

4.詹姆斯·麥迪遜（James Madison），民主共和黨，1809—1817年。

5.詹姆斯·門羅（James Monroe），民主共和黨，1817—1825年。

6.約翰·昆西·亞當斯（John Quincy Adams），民主共和黨，1825—1829年，人稱「小亞當斯」，父親是第2任美國總統，和父親是美國歷史上第一對父子檔總統。

7.安德魯·傑克遜（Andrew Jackson），民主黨，1829—1837年。

8.馬丁·范布倫（Martin Van Buren），民主黨，1837—1841年。

9.威廉·亨利·哈里森（William Henry Harrison），輝格黨，1841年上任，一個月後便死在任期內，其孫子是第23任美國總統。

10.約翰·泰勒（John Tyler），輝格黨，1841—1845 年，第一個由副總統升任總統的人。

11.詹姆斯·諾克斯·波爾克（James Knox Polk），民主黨，1845—1849年。

12.扎卡里· 泰勒（Zachary Taylor），輝格黨，1849—1850年，死於任內。

13.米勒德· 菲爾莫爾（Millard Fillmore），輝格黨，1850—1853 年，第二位由副總統升任總統的人。

14.富蘭克林· 皮爾斯（Franklin Pierce），民主黨，1853—1857年。

15.詹姆斯· 布坎南（James Buchanan），民主黨，1857—1861年。

16.亞伯拉罕· 林肯（Abraham Lincoln），共和黨，1861—1865年，任內遇刺身亡。

17.安德魯· 詹森（Andrew Johnson），民主黨，1865—1869年，任內曾遭國會的彈劾動議，以一票之差沒有通過。

18.尤利西斯· 辛普森· 格蘭特（Ulysses Simpson Grant），共和黨，1869—1877年。

19.拉瑟福德· B· 海斯（Rutherford B. Hayes），共和黨，1877—1881年。

20.詹姆斯· 加菲爾德（James Garfield），共和黨，1881年上任，半年後被暗殺，死於任內。

21.切斯特· A· 阿瑟（Chester A. Arthur），共和黨，1881—1885年。

22.格羅弗· 克里夫蘭（Stephen Grover Cleveland），民主黨，1885—1889年。

23.班傑明· 哈瑞森（Benjamin Harrison），共和黨，1889—1893 年，祖父是第9 任美國總統。

24.格羅弗· 克里夫蘭（Stephen Grover Cleveland），民主黨，1893—1897年，曾經擔任第22任美國總統，落選一屆後再度競選成功。

25.威廉· 麥金萊（William McKinley），共和黨，1897—1901年，任內遇刺身亡。

26.西奧多· 羅斯福（Theodore Roosevelt），共和黨，1901—1909年。

27.威廉· 霍華德· 塔夫脫（William Howard Taft），共和黨，1909—1913年。

28.伍德羅· 威爾遜（Woodrow Wilson），民主黨，1913—1921年。

29.沃倫· G· 哈定（Warren G.Harding），共和黨，1921—1923年，在任內去世。

30.卡爾文· 柯立芝（Calvin Coolidge），共和黨，1923—1929年。

31.赫伯特· 胡佛（Herbert Hoover），共和黨，1929—1933年。

32.富蘭克林· 德拉諾· 羅斯福（Franklin Delano Roosevelt），民主黨，1933—1945年，任期最長的美國總統，連任四屆，最後死於任內。

33.哈瑞· S· 杜魯門（Harry S. Truman），民主黨，1945—1953年。

34.德懷特· D· 艾森豪（Dwight D. Eisenhower），共和黨，1953—1961年。

35.約翰· F· 甘迺迪（John F. Kennedy），民主黨，1961—1963年，任內被暗殺。

36.林登· 詹森（Lyndon Johnson），民主黨，1963—1969年。

37.理察· 尼克森（Richard Nixon），共和黨，1969—1974年，任內因水門事件而辭職。

38.傑拉爾德· 福特（Gerald Ford），共和黨，1974—1977年，唯一一名未經選舉就接任副總統，然後又接任總統的人。

39.吉米· 卡特（Jimmy Carter），民主黨，1977—1981年。

40.隆納· 雷根（Ronald Reagan），共和黨，1981—1989年。

41.喬治· H· W· 布希（George H.W. Bush），共和黨，1989—1993年，其長子是第43任美國總統。

42.比爾· 柯林頓（Bill Clinton），民主黨，1993—2001年，任內國會曾提

起彈劾動議，但未獲通過。

43.喬治· W· 布希（George W. Bush），共和黨，2001—2009年，父親是第41任美國總統。

44.巴拉克· 歐巴馬（Barack Obama），民主黨，2009—2017年。

45.唐納· 川普（Donald John Trump），共和黨，2017—。

歷任美國總統觀察

美國開國元勛華盛頓，領導美國人民贏得獨立，制定憲法，創建國家，擔任首任總統，公眾尊稱他為「國父」、「摩西第二」。

第二任總統亞當斯，他極力贊成13州宣布獨立，並積極參與起草和領導辯論而通過《獨立宣言》，公眾尊稱他為「獨立擎天柱」、「革命建築師」。

第三任總統傑佛遜，他參與起草《獨立宣言》，當選總統之後，堅信個人權力和自由，把民主政治向前推進了一大步，公眾尊稱他為「革命鬥士」、「民主巨擘」。

第四任總統麥迪遜，他對憲法的制定、通過和批准盡力最多，公眾尊稱他為「憲法之父」。

第五任總統門羅，他是革命戰爭年代最後一位任總統的人，人們尊稱他為「革命先賢最後一人」。

第六任總統亞當斯，他是一個道德上和生活上都很嚴謹的人，人們稱其為「清教徒」。

第七任總統傑克遜，他在戰爭中立下汗馬功勞，在紐奧爾良之役打敗英軍，成為舉國聞名的英雄，當選總統後，具有領袖魅力，深受人民愛戴，被公眾尊稱為「老英雄」和「人民的總統」。

第八任總統范布倫，他從當紐約州長到協助傑克遜當選總統並出任國務卿，進而當選副總統、總統，人稱「小大人物」（身高167公分左右）、「老練政客」。

第九任總統哈里森，1811年他在印第安納州打敗肖尼印第安人，人稱「提帕卡農英雄」。

第十任總統約翰· 泰勒，美國歷史上第一位由副總統直接接任總統的人。

第十一任總統波爾克，他是美國政治歷史上第一匹「黑馬」總統候選人，任職期間孜孜不倦，人稱「黑馬波爾克」、「辛苦工作的波爾克」。

第十二任總統泰勒，他軍旅生涯40年，屢建奇功，人稱他當總統「老粗而管用」。

第十四任總統皮爾斯，他因容貌英俊，被人稱為「美男子富蘭克林」。

第十五任總統布坎南，他終身未娶，人稱「老光棍」。

第十六任總統林肯，他不矯揉造作，說話、辦事老實。1863年發布奴隸解放令，公眾尊稱他為「誠實的老亞伯」和「偉大的解放者」。

第十七任總統安德魯· 詹森，任內曾遭國會的彈劾動議，以一票之差沒有通過。

第十八任總統格蘭特，他每戰必勝，公眾稱他為「無敵尤利西斯」，又因他接受李將軍投降，結束4年內戰，被稱為「阿波麥托克斯英雄」。

第十九任總統海斯，內戰期間，他表現勇敢，數次受傷，人稱「勇敢的拉瑟福德」。

第二十任總統加菲爾德，他遵母命奮發讀書當了總統，人稱「運河少年郎總統」。

第二十一任總統阿瑟，他任內款待賓客有術，被華府社交界稱為「好客鉅子」。

第二十二任總統克里夫蘭，他公、私均極誠實，人稱「好人格羅弗」，又因在第一任4年行使414次否決權，超過從華盛頓到阿瑟21位前總統行使總和的兩倍有餘，人們戲稱他為「否決總統」。

第二十三任總統班傑明· 哈瑞森，他因維護退伍軍人權益而獲「軍人之友」的美稱。

第二十四任總統克里夫蘭，曾經擔任第22任美國總統，落選一屆後再度競選成功。

第二十五任總統麥金萊，他在總統任期間，使經濟復甦，國家繁榮，工人收入增加，人稱「繁榮的先驅」和「工人的最佳友人」。

第二十六任總統西奧多· 羅斯福，他因美西戰爭戰功卓著，而獲稱「聖胡安山英雄」。

第二十七任總統塔夫脫，他是個笑口常開，跟誰都要好的人，人們稱他為「微笑的比爾」。

第二十八任總統威爾遜，他是美國唯一一位學者從政、競選總統的人，他提出的「新自由」經濟計劃，恢復競爭，贏得人們歡心，後稱他為「學者從政」和「人民總統」。

第二十九任總統哈定，他作風平易近人，被稱為「逢人便攀談的人」。

第三十任總統柯立芝，他因謹言慎行而被稱為「謹言慎行的卡爾」。

第三十一任總統胡佛，第一次世界大戰期間，他從事國際救濟工作卓有成效，被稱為「偉大的人道主義者」。

第三十二任總統小羅斯福，他因領導第二次世界大戰取得勝利，被稱為「贏得戰爭的總統」。

第三十三任總統杜魯門，他發表杜魯門主義，面對危機從不退縮，被稱為「美國最偉大的平民總統」。

第三十四任總統艾森豪，他是五星上將，「二戰」英雄，人稱「高聳雲霄的艾森豪」。

第三十五任總統甘迺迪，他當選總統後成功解決了古巴導彈危機，被稱為「60年代風雲人物」和「林肯之後最年輕、最機智、最具領袖魅力、死後最受懷念的總統」。

第三十六任總統詹森，他被人稱為「精力充沛的德克薩斯人」。

第三十七任總統尼克森，他推動對蘇緩和，同中國關係正常化，人稱「最有爭議，最善於自我宣傳，最難捉摸的總統」。

第三十八任總統福特，他為人誠實體貼，被稱為「好好先生」，又因他當副總統和總統都不是競選的，又稱「意外副總統和意外總統」。

第三十九任總統卡特，他被稱為「讀書最勤，品行端莊，誠實無欺的總統」。

第四十任總統雷根，1981年他就職時70歲，人稱「年齡最大的總統」。

第四十一任總統布希，他獲稱為「最有外交經驗的總統」。

第四十二任總統柯林頓，他喜歡折中，不喜歡對抗，遇事繞圈子，使對方捉摸不透，被稱為「圓滑的比爾」、「唯一歷經四門（白水門、奶媽門、差旅門、州警門）而屹立不動」，最終因「拉鏈門及斯塔爾門而倒霉的總統」。

第四十三任總統小布希，他是一位遭到大毀大譽的人物，有人讚美他是「堅定有力的反恐鬥士」，有人指責他是「只會蠻幹的牛仔」。

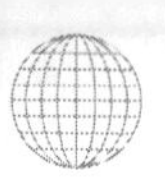

附錄二 演講名篇

一、《我有一個夢想》

I Have a Dream

Martin Luther King, Jr.

I am happy to join with you today in what will go down in history as the greatest demonstration for freedom in the history of our nation.

Five score years ago, a great American, in whose symbolic shadow we stand today, signed the Emancipation Proclamation. This momentous decree came as a great beacon light of hope to millions of Negro slaves who had been seared in the flames of withering injustice. It came as a joyous daybreak to end the long night of their captivity.

But one hundred years later, the Negro still is not free. One hundred years later, the life of the Negro is still sadly crippled by the manacles of segregation and the chains of discrimination. One hundred years later, the Negro lives on a lonely island of poverty in the midst of a vast ocean of material prosperity. One hundred years later, the Negro is still languished in the corners of American society and finds himself an exile in his own land.So we've come here today to dramatize a shameful condition.

In a sense we have come to our nation's capital to cash a check. When the architects of our republic wrote the magnificent words of the Constitution and the Declaration of Independence, they were signing a promissory note to which every

American was to fall heir. This note was a promise that all men, yes, black men as well as white men, would be guaranteed the unalienable rights of life, liberty, and the pursuit of happiness.

It is obvious today that America has defaulted on this promissory note insofar as her citizens of color are concerned. Instead of honoring this sacred obligation, America has given the Negro people a bad check, a check which has come back marked "insufficient funds". But we refuse to believe that the bank of justice is bankrupt. We refuse to believe that there are insufficient funds in the great vaults of opportunity of this nation. So we have come to cash this check, a check that will give us upon demand the riches of freedom and the security of justice. We have also come to this hallowed spot to remind America of the fierce urgency of now. This is no time to engage in the luxury of cooling off or to take the tranquilizing drug of gradualism. Now is the time to make real the promises of democracy. Now is the time to rise from the dark and desolate valley of segregation to the sunlit path of racial justice. Now is the time to lift our nation from the quick sands of racial injustice to the solid rock of brotherhood. Now is the time to make justice a reality for all of God's children.

It would be fatal for the nation to overlook the urgency of the moment. This sweltering summer of the Negro's legitimate discontent will not pass until there is an invigorating autumn of freedom and equality. Nineteen sixty-three is not an end, but a beginning. Those who hope that the Negro needed to blow off steam and will now be content will have a rude awakening if the nation returns to business as usual. There will be neither rest nor tranquility in America until the Negro is granted his citizenship rights. The whirlwinds of revolt will continue to shake the foundations of our nation until the bright day of justice emerges.

But there is something that I must say to my people who stand on the warm threshold which leads into the palace of justice. In the process of gaining our rightful place we must not be guilty of wrongful deeds. Let us not seek to satisfy our thirst for freedom by drinking from the cup of bitterness and hatred.

We must forever conduct our struggle on the high plane of dignity and discipline. We must not allow our creative protest to degenerate into physical violence. Again and again we must rise to the majestic heights of meeting physical force with soul force. The marvelous new militancy which has engulfed the Negro community must not lead us to a distrust of all white people, for many of our white brothers, as evidenced by their presence here today, have come to realize that their destiny is tied up with our destiny. They have come to realize that their freedom is inextricably bound to our freedom. We cannot walk alone.

As we walk, we must make the pledge that we shall always march ahead. We cannot turn back. There are those who are asking the devotees of civil rights, "When will you be satisfied?" We can never be satisfied as long as the Negro is the victim of the unspeakable horrors of police brutality. We can never be satisfied, as long as our bodies, heavy with the fatigue of travel, cannot gain lodging in the motels of the highways and the hotels of the cities. We cannot be satisfied as long as the Negro's basic mobility is from a smaller ghetto to a larger one. We can never be satisfied as long as our children are stripped of their selfhood and robbed of their dignity by signs stating "For Whites Only". We cannot be satisfied as long as a Negro in Mississippi cannot vote and a Negro in New York believes he has nothing for which to vote. No, no, we are not satisfied, and we will not be satisfied until justice rolls down like waters and righteousness like a mighty stream.

I am not unmindful that some of you have come here out of great trials and tribulations. Some of you have come fresh from narrow jail cells. Some of you have come from areas where your quest for freedom left you battered by the storms of persecution and staggered by the winds of police brutality. You have been the veterans of creative suffering. Continue to work with the faith that unearned suffering is redemptive.

Go back to Mississippi, go back to Alabama, go back to South Carolina, go back to Georgia, go back to Louisiana, go back to the slums and ghettos of our northern cities, knowing that somehow this situation can and will be changed. Let us not wallow in the valley of despair. I say to you today, my friends.

So even though we face the difficulties of today and tomorrow, I still have a dream. It is a dream deeply rooted in the American dream.

I have a dream that one day this nation will rise up and live out the true meaning of its creed: "We hold these truths to be self-evident, that all men are created equal."

I have a dream that one day on the red hills of Georgia the sons of former slaves and the sons of former slave-owners will be able to sit down together at the table of brotherhood.

I have a dream that one day even the state of Mississippi, a state sweltering with the heat of injustice, sweltering with the heat of oppression, will be transformed into an oasis of freedom and justice.

I have a dream that my four children will one day live in a nation where they will not be judged by the color of their skin but by the content of their character.

I have a dream today!

I have a dream that one day, down in Alabama, with its vicious racists, with its governor having his lips dripping with the words of interposition and nullification, one day right there in Alabama little black boys and black girls will be able to join hands with little white boys and white girls as sisters and brothers.

I have a dream today!

I have a dream that one day every valley shall be exalted, every hill and mountain shall be made low, the rough places will be made plain, and the crooked places will be made straight, and the glory of the Lord shall be revealed, and all flesh shall see it together.

This is our hope. This is the faith that I go back to the South with. With this faith we will be able to hew out of the mountain of despair a stone of hope. With this faith we will be able to transform the jangling discords of our nation into a beautiful symphony of brotherhood. With this faith we will be able to work together, to pray together, to struggle together, to go to jail together, to stand up for freedom together, knowing that we will be free one day.

This will be the day when all of God's children will be able to sing with new meaning.

My country, 'tis of thee,

Sweet land of liberty,

Of thee I sing:

Land where my fathers died,

Land of the pilgrims' pride,

From every mountainside,

Let freedom ring.

And if America is to be a great nation this must become true.

And So let freedom ring from the prodigious hilltops of New Hampshire!

Let freedom ring from the mighty mountains of New York!

Let freedom ring from the heightening Alleghenies of Pennsylvania!

Let freedom ring from the snowcapped Rockies of Colorado!

Let freedom ring from the curvaceous slops of California!

But not only that;

let freedom ring from Stone Mountain of Georgia!

Let freedom ring from Lookout Mountain of Tennessee!

Let freedom ring from every hill and molehill of Mississippi!

From every mountainside, let freedom ring!

And when this happens, when we allow freedom ring, when we let it ring from every village and every hamlet, from every state and every city, we will be able to speed up that day when all of God's children, black men and white men, Jews and Gentiles, Protestants and Catholics, will be able to join hands and sing in the words of the old Negro spiritual, "Free at last! Free at last! Thank God Almighty, we are free at last!"

二、蓋茲堡演説

【中文簡介】

《蓋茲堡演説》（Gettysburg Address）是亞伯拉罕· 林肯最著名的演説，也是美國歷史上為人引用最多的政治性演説。1863年11月19日，正值美國內戰中蓋茲堡戰役結束後四個半月，林肯在賓夕法尼亞州蓋茲堡的蓋茲堡國家公墓（Gettysburg National Cemetery）揭幕式中發表該演説，哀悼在長達五個半月的蓋茲堡戰役中陣亡的將士。林肯的演講於當天第二順位發表，修辭細膩周密，其後成為美國歷史上最偉大的演説之一。以不足三百字的字數，在兩三分鐘的時間裡，林肯訴諸《獨立宣言》所支持的人生而平等的原則，並重新定義這場內戰：不止是為聯邦存續而奮鬥，更是「自由之新生」，將真正的平等帶給全體公民。

演説以「八十七年前」發端，林肯論及美國獨立革命，稱許蓋茲堡這場揭幕式為一契機，不只是獻一塊墓地，更能藉此尊崇殊死搏鬥以確保「民有、民治、民享之政府當免於凋零」的將士們。

出乎意料的是，儘管這場演說名垂青史，聲震寰宇，其具體措辭卻頗受爭議。五份已知的演說稿，與當時新聞報導中的謄抄本，在若干細節上彼此互異。

在眾多版本中，「畢利斯本」（Bliss Copy）已成標準本。這是唯一一份林肯署名的版本，也是所知經其撰寫的最終版本。（以下為此版本的中英對照）

【中英對照】

Gettysburg Address

Abraham Lincoln

Four score and seven years ago our fathers brought forth on this continent, a new nation, conceived in Liberty, and dedicated to the proposition that all men are created equal.

Now we are engaged in a great civil war, testing whether that nation or any nation so conceived and so dedicated, can long endure. We are met on a great battle field of that war. We have come to dedicate a portion of that field, as a final resting place for those who here gave their lives that that nation might live. It is altogether fitting and proper that we should do this.

But, in a larger sense, we can not dedicate — we can not consecrate — we can not hallow — this ground. The brave men, living and dead, who struggled here, have consecrated it, far above our poor power to add or detract. The world will little note, nor long remember what we say here, but it can never forget what they did here. It is for us the living, rather, to be dedicated here to the unfinished work which they who fought here have thus far so nobly advanced. It is rather for us to be here dedicated to the great task remaining before us — that from these honored dead we take increased devotion to that cause for which they gave the last full measure of devotion — that we here highly resolve that these dead shall not have died in vain — that this nation, under God, shall have a new birth of freedom — and that government of the people, by the people, for the people, shall not perish from the earth.

八十又七年前吾輩先祖於這大陸上，肇建一個新的國度，乃孕育於自由，且致力於凡人皆生而平等之信念。

當下吾等被捲入一場偉大的內戰，以考驗是否此國度，或任何肇基於和奉獻於斯者，可永垂不朽。吾等現相逢於此戰中一處浩大戰場。而吾等將奉獻此戰場之部分，作為這群交付彼者生命讓那國度勉能生存的人們最後安息之處。此乃全然妥切且適當而為吾人應行之舉。

但，於更大意義之上，吾等無法致力、無法奉上、無法成就此土之聖。這群勇者，無論生死，曾於斯奮戰到底，早已使其神聖，而遠超過吾人卑微之力所能增減。這世間不曾絲毫留意，也不長久記得吾等於斯所言，但永不忘懷彼人於此所為。吾等生者，理應當然，獻身於此輩鞠躬盡瘁之未完大業。吾等在此責無旁貸獻身於眼前之偉大使命：自光榮的亡者之處吾人肩起其終極之奉獻——吾等在此答應亡者之死當非徒然——此國度，於神佑之下，當享有自由之新生——民有、民治、民享之政府當免於凋零。

三、巴拉克· 歐巴馬的就職演講

fanuary 20, 2009, Barack Obama has been sworn in as the 44th US president. Here is his inauguration speech in full.

My fellow citizens:

I stand here today humbled by the task before us, grateful for the trust you have bestowed, mindful of the sacrifices borne by our ancestors. I thank President Bush for his service to our nation, as well as the generosity and cooperation he has shown throughout this transition.

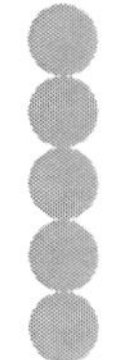

Forty-four Americans have now taken the presidential oath. The words have been spoken during rising tides of prosperity and the still waters of peace. Yet, every so often the oath is taken amidst gathering clouds and raging storms.

At these moments, America has carried on not simply because of the skill or vision of those in high office, but because we, the people, have remained faithful to the ideals of our forbearers, and true to our founding documents.

So it has been. So it must be with this generation of Americans.

Serious Challenges

That we are in the midst of crisis is now well understood. Our nation is at war, against a far-reaching network of violence and hatred. Our economy is badly weakened, a consequence of greed and irresponsibility on the part of some, but also our collective failure to make hard choices and prepare the nation for a new age. Homes have been lost; jobs shed; businesses shuttered. Our healthcare is too costly; our schools fail too many; and each day brings further evidence that the ways we use energy strengthen our adversaries and threaten our planet.

These are the indicators of crisis, subject to data and statistics. Less measurable but no less profound is a sapping of confidence across our land — a nagging fear that America's decline is inevitable, that the next generation must lower its sights.

Today I say to you that the challenges we face are real. They are serious and they are many. They will not be met easily or in a short span of time. But know this, America — they will be met.

On this day, we gather because we have chosen hope over fear, unity of purpose over conflict and discord.

On this day, we come to proclaim an end to the petty grievances and false promises, the recriminations and worn-out dogmas, that for far too long have strangled our politics.

Nation of "Risk-takers"

We remain a young nation, but in the words of scripture, the time has come to

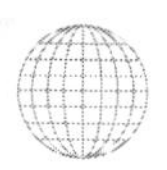

set aside childish things. The time has come to reaffirm our enduring spirit; to choose our better history; to carry forward that precious gift, that noble idea, passed on from generation to generation: the God-given promise that all are equal, all are free, and all deserve a chance to pursue their full measure of happiness.

In reaffirming the greatness of our nation, we understand that greatness is never a given. It must be earned. Our journey has never been one of short-cuts or settling for less. It has not been the path for the faint-hearted — for those who prefer leisure over work, or seek only the pleasures of riches and fame. Rather, it has been the risktakers, the doers, the makers of things — some celebrated but more often men and women obscure in their labor, who have carried us up the long, rugged path towards prosperity and freedom.

For us, they packed up their few worldly possessions and travelled across oceans in search of a new life.

For us, they toiled in sweatshops and settled the West; endured the lash of the whip and plowed the hard earth.

For us, they fought and died, in places like Concord and Gettysburg, Normandy and Khe Sahn.

Remaking America

Time and again these men and women struggled and sacrificed and worked till their hands were raw so that we might live a better life. They saw America as bigger than the sum of our individual ambitions; greater than all the differences of birth or wealth or faction.

This is the journey we continue today. We remain the most prosperous, powerful nation on Earth. Our workers are no less productive than when this crisis began. Our minds are no less inventive, our goods and services no less needed than they were last week or last month or last year. Our capacity remains undiminished.

But our time of standing pat, of protecting narrow interests and putting off unpleasant decisions — that time has surely passed. Starting today, we must pick ourselves up, dust ourselves off, and begin again the work of remaking America.

For everywhere we look, there is work to be done. The state of our economy calls for action, bold and swift, and we will act not only to create new jobs, but to lay a new foundation for growth. We will build the roads and bridges, the electric grids and digital lines that feed our commerce and bind us together. We will restore science to its rightful place, and wield technology's wonders to raise healthcare's quality and lower its cost. We will harness the sun and the winds and the soil to fuel our cars and run our factories. And we will transform our schools and colleges and universities to meet the demands of a new age. All this we can do.All this we will do.

Restoring Trust

Now, there are some who question the scale of our ambitions — who suggest that our system cannot tolerate too many big plans. Their memories are short. For they have forgotten what this country has already done; what free men and women can achieve when imagination is joined to common purpose, and necessity to courage.

What the cynics fail to understand is that the ground has shifted beneath them — that the stale political arguments that have consumed us for so long no longer apply.

The question we ask today is not whether our government is too big or too small, but whether it works — whether it helps families find jobs at a decent wage, care they can afford, a retirement that is dignified. Where the answer is yes, we intend to move forward. Where the answer is no, programmes will end. And those of us who manage the public's dollars will be held to account — to spend wisely, reform bad habits, and do our business in the light of day — because only then can we restore the vital trust between a people and their government.

Nor is the question before us whether the market is a force for good or ill. Its power to generate wealth and expand freedom is unmatched, but this crisis has reminded us that without a watchful eye, the market can spin out of control — that a nation cannot prosper long when it favors only the prosperous. The success of our economy has always depended not just on the size of our gross domestic product, but on the reach of our prosperity; on the ability to extend opportunity to every willing heart — not out of charity, but because it is the surest route to our common good.

Ready to Lead

As for our common defense, we reject as false the choice between our safety and our ideals. Our founding fathers, faced with perils that we can scarcely imagine, drafted a charter to assure the rule of law and the rights of man, a charter expanded by the blood of generations. Those ideals still light the world, and we will not give them up for expedience's sake. And so to all the other peoples and governments who are watching today, from the grandest capitals to the small village where my father was born: know that America is a friend of each nation and every man, woman, and child who seeks a future of peace and dignity, and we are ready to lead once more.

Recall that earlier generations faced down fascism and communism not just with missiles and tanks, but with the sturdy alliances and enduring convictions. They understood that our power alone cannot protect us, nor does it entitle us to do as we please. Instead, they knew that our power grows through its prudent use; our security emanates from the justness of our cause, the force of our example, the tempering qualities of humility and restraint.

We are the keepers of this legacy. Guided by these principles once more, we can meet those new threats that demand even greater effort — even greater cooperation and understanding between nations. We will begin to responsibly leave

Iraq to its people, and forge a hard-earned peace in Afghanistan. With old friends and former foes, we will work tirelessly to lessen the nuclear threat, and roll back the specter of a warming planet. We will not apologize for our way of life, nor will we waver in its defense, and for those who seek to advance their aims by inducing terror and slaughtering innocents, we say to you now that our spirit is stronger and cannot be broken; you cannot outlast us, and we will defeat you.

Era of Peace

For we know that our patchwork heritage is a strength, not a weakness. We are a nation of Christians and Muslims, Jews and Hindus — and non-believers. We are shaped by every language and culture, drawn from every end of this earth; and because we have tasted the bitter swill of civil war and segregation, and emerged from that dark chapter stronger and more united, we cannot help but believe that the old hatreds shall someday pass; that the lines of tribe shall soon dissolve; that as the world grows smaller, our common humanity shall reveal itself; and that America must play its role in ushering in a new era of peace.

To the Muslim world, we seek a new way forward, based on mutual interest and mutual respect. To those leaders around the globe who seek to sow conflict, or blame their society's ills on the West — know that your people will judge you on what you can build, not what you destroy. To those who cling to power through corruption and deceit and the silencing of dissent, know that you are on the wrong side of history; but that we will extend a hand if you are willing to unclench your fist.

To the people of poor nations, we pledge to work alongside you to make your farms flourish and let clean waters flow; to nourish starved bodies and feed hungry minds. And to those nations like ours that enjoy relative plenty, we say we can no longer afford indifference to the suffering outside our borders; nor can we consume the world's resources without regard to effect. For the world has changed, and we

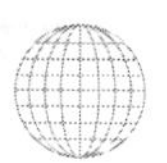

must change with it.

Duties

As we consider the road that unfolds before us, we remember with humble gratitude those brave Americans who, at this very hour, patrol far-off deserts and distant mountains. They have something to tell us today, just as the fallen heroes who lie in Arlington whisper through the ages. We honor them not only because they are the guardians of our liberty, but because they embody the spirit of service; a willingness to find meaning in something greater than themselves. And yet, at this moment — a moment that will define a generation — it is precisely this spirit that must inhabit us all.

For as much as government can do and must do, it is ultimately the faith and determination of the American people upon which this nation relies. It is the kindness to take in a stranger when the levees break, the selflessness of workers who would rather cut their hours than see a friend lose their job which sees us through our darkest hours. It is the firefighter's courage to storm a stairway filled with smoke, but also a parent's willingness to nurture a child, that finally decides our fate.

Our challenges may be new. The instruments with which we meet them may be new. But those values upon which our success depend — honesty and hard work, courage and fair play, tolerance and curiosity, loyalty and patriotism — these things are old. These things are true. They have been the quiet force of progress throughout our history. What is demanded then is a return to these truths.

What is required of us now is a new era of responsibility — a recognition, on the part of every American, that we have duties to ourselves, our nation, and the world, duties that we do not grudgingly accept but rather seize gladly, firm in the knowledge that there is nothing so satisfying to the spirit, so defining of our character, than giving our all to a difficult task.

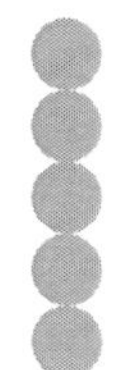

Gift of Freedom

This is the price and the promise of citizenship.

This is the source of our confidence — the knowledge that God calls on us to shape an uncertain destiny.

This is the meaning of our liberty and our creed — why men and women and children of every race and every faith can join in celebration across this magnificent mall, and why a man whose father less than 60 years ago might not have been served at a local restaurant can now stand before you to take a most sacred oath.

So let us mark this day with remembrance, of who we are and how far we have travelled. In the year of America's birth, in the coldest of months, a small band of patriots huddled by dying campfires on the shores of an icy river. The capital was abandoned. The enemy was advancing. The snow was stained with blood. At a moment when the outcome of our revolution was most in doubt, the father of our nation ordered these words be read to the people:

"Let it be told to the future world... that in the depth of winter, when nothing but hope and virtue could survive... that the city and the country, alarmed at one common danger, came forth to meet (it)."

America. In the face of our common dangers, in this winter of our hardship, let us remember these timeless words. With hope and virtue, let us brave once more the icy currents, and endure what storms may come. Let it be said by our children's children that when we were tested we refused to let this journey end, that we did not turn back nor did we falter; and with eyes fixed on the horizon and God's grace upon us, we carried forth that great gift of freedom and delivered it safely to future generations.

Thank you. God bless you. And God bless the United States of America.

四、《熱血、汗水和眼淚》

【英文原文】

Blood, Sweat and Tears

Winston Churchill

(May 13, 1940)

On Friday evening last I received from His Majesty the mission to form a new administration.

It was the evident will of Parliament and the nation that this should be conceived on the broadest possible basis and that it should include all parties.

I have already completed the most important part of this task. A war cabinet has been formed of five members, representing, with the Labor, Opposition and Liberals, the unity of the nation.

It was necessary that this should be done in one single day on account of the extreme urgency and rigor of events. Other key positions were filled yesterday. I am submitting a further list to the king tonight. I hope to complete the appointment of principal ministers during tomorrow.

The appointment of other ministers usually takes a little longer. I trust when Parliament meets again this part of my task will be completed and that the administration will be complete in all respects.

I considered it in the public interest to suggest to the Speaker that the House should be summoned today. At the end of today's proceedings, the adjournment of the House will be proposed until May 21 with provision for earlier meeting if need be. Business for that will be notified to MPs at the earliest opportunity.

I now invite the House by a resolution to record its approval of the steps taken and declare its confidence in the new government. The resolution:

"That this House welcomes the formation of a government representing the united and inflexible resolve of the nation to prosecute the war with Germany to a victorious conclusion."

To form an administration of this scale and complexity is a serious undertaking in itself. But we are in the preliminary phase of one of the greatest battles in history. We are in action at many other points — in Norway and in Holland — and we have to be prepared in the Mediterranean. The air battle is continuing, and many preparations have to be made here at home.

In this crisis I think I may be pardoned if I do not address the House at any length today, and I hope that any of my friends and colleagues or former colleagues who are affected by the political reconstruction will make all allowances for any lack of ceremony with which it has been necessary to act.

I say to the House as I said to ministers who have joined this government, I have nothing to offer but blood, toil, tears and sweat. We have before us an ordeal of the most grievous kind. We have before us many, many months of struggle and suffering.

You ask, what is our policy? I say it is to wage war by land, sea and air. War with all our might and with all the strength God has given us, and to wage war against a monstrous tyranny never surpassed in the dark and lamentable catalogue of human crime. That is our policy.

You ask, what is our aim? I can answer in one word. It is victory. Victory at all costs — victory in spite of all terrors — victory, however long and hard the road may be, for without victory there is no survival.

Let that be realized. No survival for the British Empire, no survival for all that the British Empire has stood for, no survival for the urge, the impulse of the ages, that mankind shall move forward toward his goal.

I take up my task in buoyancy and hope. I feel sure that our cause will not be suffered to fail among men.

I feel entitled at this juncture, at this time, to claim the aid of all and to say, "Come then, let us go forward together with our united strength."

【中文譯文】

熱血、汗水和眼淚

溫斯頓· 邱吉爾

上星期五晚上，我奉陛下之命，組織新一屆的政府。

按國會和國民的意願，新政府顯然應該考慮建立在盡可能廣泛的基礎上，應該兼容所有的黨派。

我已經完成了這項任務最主要的部分。戰時內閣由五人組成，包括工黨、反對黨和自由黨，這體現了舉國團結一致。

由於事態極端緊急和嚴峻，新政府須於一天之內組成，其他的關鍵崗位也於昨日安排就緒。今晚還要向國王呈報一份名單。我希望明天就能完成幾位主要大臣的任命。

其餘大臣們的任命照例得晚一些。我相信，在國會下一次召開時，任命將告完成，並臻於完善。

為公眾利益著想，我建議議長今天就召開國會。今天的議程結束時，建議休會到5月21日，並準備在必要時提前開會。有關事項當會及早通知各位議員。

現在我請求國會作出決議，批准我所採取的各項步驟，並且聲明對新政府的信任。決議如下：

「本國會歡迎新政府的組成，新政府體現了舉國一致的堅定不移的決心：對德作戰，直到最後勝利。」

組織如此規模和如此複雜的政府原本是一項重大的任務。但是我們正處於歷史上罕見的一場大戰的初始階段。我們在其他許多地方都有戰場——在挪威，在荷蘭，我們還必須在地中海做好準備。空戰正在繼續，而且在本土也必須做好許多準備工作。

值此危急關頭，我想，即使我今天向國會作的報告過於簡略，也當能見諒。我還希望所有在這次改組中受到影響的朋友、同僚和舊日的同僚們，對禮儀方面的任何不周之處能夠理解。

我向國會表明，正如我向入閣的大臣們所表明的，我所能奉獻的唯有熱血、辛勞、眼淚和汗水。我們所面臨的將是一場極其嚴酷的考驗，將是曠日持久的鬥爭和苦難。

若問我們的政策是什麼？我的回答是：在陸上、海上、空中作戰。盡我們的全力，用上帝賦予我們的全部力量去戰鬥，對人類黑暗、可悲的罪惡史上空前兇殘的暴政作戰。這就是我們的政策。

若問我們的目標是什麼？我可以用一個詞來回答，那就是勝利。不惜一切代價，去奪取勝利——不懼一切恐怖，去奪取勝利——不論前面的路如何漫長、如何艱苦，都要奪取勝利。因為沒有勝利就不能生存。

我們務必認識到，沒有勝利大英帝國將不復存在，沒有勝利大英帝國所象徵的一切將不復存在，沒有勝利多少世紀以來的強烈要求和衝動將不復存在；人類應當向自己的目標邁進。

我精神振奮、滿懷信心地承擔起我的任務。我確信，大家聯合起來，我們的事業就不會遭到挫敗。

在此時此刻的危急關頭，我覺得我有權要求各方面的支持。我要說：「來吧，讓我們群策群力，並肩前進！」

五、賈伯斯在史丹佛大學的演講

【英文原文】

Stay Hungry, Stay Foolish

Steve Jobs

This is the text of the Commencement address by Steve Jobs, CEO of Apple Computer and of Pixar Animation Studios, delivered on June 12, 2005.

I am honored to be with you today at your commencement from one of the finest universities in the world. I never graduated from college. Truth be told, this is the closest I've ever gotten to a college graduation. Today I want to tell you three stories from my life. That's it. No big deal.Just three stories.

The first story is about connecting the dots.

I dropped out of Reed College after the first 6 months, but then stayed around as a drop-in for another 18 months or so before I really quit. So why did I drop out?

It started before I was born. My biological mother was a young, unwed college graduate student, and she decided to put me up for adoption. She felt very strongly that I should be adopted by college graduates, so everything was all set for me to be adopted at birth by a lawyer and his wife. Except that when I popped out they decided at the last minute that they really wanted a girl. So my parents, who were on a waiting list, got a call in the middle of the night asking: "We have an unexpected baby boy; do you want him?" They said: "Of course." My biological mother later found out that my mother had never graduated from college and that my father had never graduated from high school. She refused to sign the final adoption papers. She only relented a few months later when my parents promised that I would someday go to college.

And 17 years later I did go to college. But I naively chose a college that was almost as expensive as Stanford, and all of my working-class parents' savings were being spent on my college tuition. After six months, I couldn't see the value in it. I had no idea what I wanted to do with my life and no idea how college was going to help me figure it out. And here I was spending all of the money my parents had saved their entire life. So I decided to drop out and trust that it would all work out OK. It was pretty scary at the time, but looking back it was one of the best decisions I ever made. The minute I dropped out I could stop taking the required classes that didn't interest me, and begin dropping in on the ones that looked interesting.

It wasn't all romantic. I didn't have a dorm room, so I slept on the floor in friends' rooms, I returned coke bottles for the 5 cents deposits to buy food with, and I would walk the 7 miles across town every Sunday night to get one good meal a week at the Hare Krishna temple. I loved it. And much of what I stumbled into by following my curiosity and intuition turned out to be priceless later on. Let me give you one example:

Reed College at that time offered perhaps the best calligraphy instruction in the country. Throughout the campus every poster, every label on every drawer, was beautifully hand calligraphed. Because I had dropped out and didn't have to take the normal classes, I decided to take a calligraphy class to learn how to do this. I learned about serif and san serif typefaces, about varying the amount of space between different letter combinations, about what makes great typography great. It was beautiful, historical, artistically subtle in a way that science can't capture, and I found it fascinating.

None of this had even a hope of any practical application in my life. But ten years later, when we were designing the first Macintosh computer, it all came back to me. And we designed it all into the Mac. It was the first computer with beautiful typography. If I had never dropped in on that single course in college, the Mac would have never had multiple typefaces or proportionally spaced fonts. And since Windows just copied the Mac, it's likely that no personal computer would have

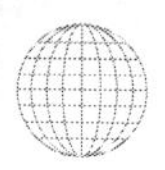

them. If I had never dropped out, I would have never dropped in on this calligraphy class, and personal computers might not have the wonderful typography that they do. Of course it was impossible to connect the dots looking forward when I was in college. But it was very, very clear looking backwards ten years later.

Again, you can't connect the dots looking forward; you can only connect them looking backwards. So you have to trust that the dots will somehow connect in your future. You have to trust in something — your gut, destiny, life, karma, whatever. This approach has never let me down, and it has made all the difference in my life.

My second story is about love and loss.

I was lucky — I found what I loved to do early in life. Woz and I started Apple in my parents' garage when I was 20. We worked hard, and in 10 years Apple had grown from just the two of us in a garage into a $ 2 billion company with over 4,000 employees. We had just released our finest creation — the Macintosh — a year earlier, and I had just turned 30. And then I got fired. How can you get fired from a company you started? Well, as Apple grew we hired someone who I thought was very talented to run the company with me, and for the first year or so things went well. But then our visions of the future began to diverge and eventually we had a falling out. When we did, our Board of Directors sided with him. So at 30 I was out. And very publicly out. What had been the focus of my entire adult life was gone, and it was devastating.

I really didn't know what to do for a few months. I felt that I had let the previous generation of entrepreneurs down — that I had dropped the baton as it was being passed to me. I met with David Packard and Bob Noyce and tried to apologize for screwing up so badly. I was a very public failure, and I even thought about running away from the valley. But something slowly began to dawn on me — I still loved what I did. The turn of events at Apple had not changed that one bit. I had been rejected, but I was still in love. And so I decided to start over.

I didn't see it then, but it turned out that getting fired from Apple was the best thing that could have ever happened to me. The heaviness of being successful was replaced by the lightness of being a beginner again, less sure about everything. It freed me to enter one of the most creative periods of my life.

During the next five years, I started a company named NeXT, another company named Pixar, and fell in love with an amazing woman who would become my wife. Pixar went on to create the world's first computer animated feature film, Toy Story, and is now the most successful animation studio in the world. In a remarkable turn of events, Apple bought NeXT, I returned to Apple, and the technology we developed at NeXT is at the heart of Apple's current renaissance. And Laurene and I have a wonderful family together.

I'm pretty sure none of this would have happened if I hadn't been fired from Apple. It was awful tasting medicine, but I guess the patient needed it. Sometimes life hits you in the head with a brick. Don't lose faith. I'm convinced that the only thing that kept me going was that I loved what I did. You've got to find what you love. And that is as true for your work as it is for your lovers. Your work is going to fill a large part of your life, and the only way to be truly satisfied is to do what you believe is great work. And the only way to do great work is to love what you do. If you haven't found it yet, keep looking. Don't settle. As with all matters of the heart, you'll know when you find it. And, like any great relationship, it just gets better and better as the years roll on. So keep looking until you find it. Don't settle.

My third story is about death.

When I was 17, I read a quote that went something like" "If you live each day as if it was your last, someday you'll most certainly be right." It made an impression on me, and since then, for the past 33 years, I have looked in the mirror every morning and asked myself: "If today were the last day of my life, would I want to do what I am about to do today?" And whenever the answer has been "No" for too many days in a row, I know I need to change something.

Remembering that I'll be dead soon is the most important tool I've ever encountered to help me make the big choices in life. Because almost everything — all external expectations, all pride, all fear of embarrassment or failure — these things just fall away in the face of death, leaving only what is truly important. Remembering that you are going to die is the best way I know to avoid the trap of thinking you have something to lose. You are already naked. There is no reason not to follow your heart.

About a year ago I was diagnosed with cancer. I had a scan at 7:30 in the morning, and it clearly showed a tumor on my pancreas. I didn't even know what a pancreas was. The doctors told me this was almost certainly a type of cancer that is incurable, and that I should expect to live no longer than three to six months. My doctor advised me to go home and get my affairs in order, which is doctor's code for prepare to die. It means to try to tell your kids everything you thought you'd have the next 10 years to tell them in just a few months. It means to make sure everything is buttoned up so that it will be as easy as possible for your family. It means to say your goodbyes.

I lived with that diagnosis all day. Later that evening I had a biopsy, where they stuck an endoscope down my throat, through my stomach and into my intestines, put a needle into my pancreas and got a few cells from the tumor. I was sedated, but my wife, who was there, told me that when they viewed the cells under a microscope the doctors started crying because it turned out to be a very rare form of pancreatic cancer that is curable with surgery. I had the surgery and I'm fine now.

This was the closest I've been to facing death, and I hope it's the closest I get for a few more decades. Having lived through it, I can now say this to you with a bit more certainty than when death was a useful but purely intellectual concept:

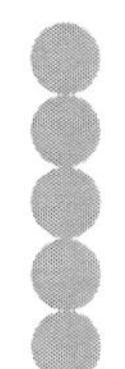

No one wants to die. Even people who want to go to heaven don't want to die to get there. And yet death is the destination we all share. No one has ever escaped it. And that is as it should be, because Death is very likely the single best invention of Life. It is Life's change agent. It clears out the old to make way for the new. Right now the new is you, but someday not too long from now, you will gradually become the old and be cleared away. Sorry to be so dramatic, but it is quite true.

Your time is limited, so don't waste it living someone else's life. Don't be trapped by dogma — which is living with the results of other people's thinking. Don't let the noise of others' opinions drown out your own inner voice. And most important, have the courage to follow your heart and intuition. They somehow already know what you truly want to become. Everything else is secondary.

When I was young, there was an amazing publication called The Whole Earth Catalog, which was one of the bibles of my generation. It was created by a fellow named Stewart Brand not far from here in Menlo Park, and he brought it to life with his poetic touch. This was in the late 1960's, before personal computers and desktop publishing, so it was all made with typewriters, scissors, and polaroid cameras. It was sort of like Google in paperback form, 35 years before Google came along: it was idealistic, and overflowing with neat tools and great notions.

Stewart and his team put out several issues of The Whole Earth Catalog, and then when it had run its course, they put out a final issue. It was the mid-1970s, and I was your age. On the back cover of their final issue was a photograph of an early morning country road, the kind you might find yourself hitchhiking on if you were so adventurous. Beneath it were the words: "Stay Hungry. Stay Foolish." It was their farewell message as they signed off. Stay Hungry. Stay Foolish. And I have always wished that for myself. And now, as you graduate to begin anew, I wish that for you. Stay Hungry. Stay Foolish.

Thank you all very much.

【中文譯文】

求知若饑，虛心若愚

史蒂夫· 賈伯斯

這是蘋果公司和皮克斯動畫公司總裁史蒂夫· 賈伯斯2005年6月12日在史丹佛大學畢業典禮上的演講。

今天，很榮幸來到各位從世界上最好的學校之一畢業的畢業典禮上。我從來沒從大學畢業。說實話，這是我離大學畢業最近的一刻。今天，我只說三個故事，不談大道理，三個故事就好。

第一個故事，是關於人生中的點點滴滴怎麼串聯在一起。

我在里德學院待了六個月就辦了休學。到我退學前，一共休學了十八個月。那麼，我為什麼要休學呢？

這得從我出生前講起。我的親生母親當時是個研究生，年輕未婚媽媽，她決定讓別人收養我。她堅決認為應該讓上過大學的人收養我，所以她就準備我一出生就由一對律師夫婦收養。但是這對夫妻到了最後一刻反悔了，他們想收養個女孩。

所以在等待收養名單上的一對夫妻，我的養父母，在一天半夜裡接到一通電話，問他們「有一名意外出生的男孩，你們要認養他嗎？」而他們的回答是「當然要」。後來，我的生母發現，我現在的媽媽根本沒有大學畢業，我現在的爸爸則連高中都沒畢業。她拒絕在最終的收養文件上簽字。直到幾個月後，我的養父母同意將來一定會讓我上大學，她才勉強答應了。

十七年後，我上大學了。但是當時我天真地選了一所學費幾乎跟史丹佛大學一樣貴的大學，我的父母都是工薪階層，把所有積蓄都花在我的學費上了。六個月後，我看不出念這個書的價值何在。那時候，我不知道這輩子要幹什麼，也不知道念大學能對我有什麼幫助，而且我為了念這個書，花光了我父母這輩子的所有積蓄。

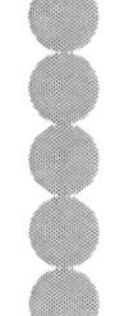

所以我決定休學，相信船到橋頭自然直。當時這個決定看來相當可怕，可是現在看來，那是我這輩子做過的最好的決定之一。休學之後，我再也不用上我沒興趣的必修課，可以把時間用來聽那些自己感興趣的課。

這一點也不浪漫。我沒有宿舍，所以就睡在朋友們家裡的地板上，靠回收可樂空罐來掙那五先令退費來買吃的，每個星期天晚上得走七英里路繞過大半個鎮子去印度教的Hare Krishna神廟吃頓好的。我喜歡Hare Krishna神廟的好吃的。追尋著自己的好奇與直覺，我花時間做的大部分事，後來看來都成了無價之寶。舉例來說：

當時里德學院有著大概是全國最好的書法課程。校園內的每一張海報上，每個抽屜的標籤上，都是美麗的手寫字。因為我休學了，可以不照正常選課程序來，所以我就跑去學書法。我學了serif 與san serif 字體，學會了在不同字母組合間變更字間距，體會到了排版的偉大之處。書法的美好、歷史感與藝術感是科學所無法捕捉的，我覺得那很迷人。

我沒想過學這些東西能在我生活中起些什麼實際作用，不過十年後，當我在設計第一台麥金塔時，我想起了當時所學的東西，所以把這些東西都設計進了麥金塔裡，這是第一台能印刷出漂亮字體的電腦。如果我沒沉溺於那樣一門課裡，麥金塔可能就不會有多重字體跟變間距字體了。又因為Windows抄襲了麥金塔的使用方式，如果當年我沒這樣做，大概世界上所有的個人電腦都不會有這些東西，印不出現在我們看到的漂亮的字來了。當然，當我還在大學裡時，不可能把這些點點滴滴預先串在一起，但是十年後回顧起來，就顯得非常清楚。我再說一次，你不能預先把點點滴滴串在一起；唯有在未來回顧時，你才會明白那些點點滴滴是如何串在一起的。

所以你得相信，你現在所經歷的，將來總會連接在一塊。你得信任些什麼，直覺也好，命運也好，生命也好，因緣也好，或是其他什麼也好。這種做法從來沒讓我失望，也使我的整個人生變得不同。

我的第二個故事，有關愛與失去。

我很幸運，年輕時就找到了自己喜歡做的事。二十歲時，我跟Woz一起在我爸媽的車庫裡開始了蘋果的事業。我們拚命工作，蘋果在十年間從一間車庫裡的兩個小夥子擴展成了一家員工超過四千人、市價二十億美金的公司，而且在那之前那年就推出了我們最棒的作品——麥金塔。當時我才剛邁入人生的第三十個年頭，但隨後卻被炒了魷魚。

自己創辦的公司怎麼會炒自己魷魚？

是這樣的，當蘋果逐漸成長後，我請了一個在經營公司上很有才幹的傢伙來，他在頭幾年也確實幹得不錯。可是我們對未來的願景不同，最後只好分道揚鑣，而董事會站在他那邊，炒了我魷魚，公開把我請了出去。曾經是我整個成年生活重心的東西不見了，令我不知所措。有幾個月，我實在不知道要幹什麼好。我覺得我令企業界的前輩們失望了，我把他們交給我的接力棒弄丟了。我見到創辦 HP 的David Packard跟創辦Intel 的Bob Noyce時，跟他們說我很抱歉把事情搞砸了。我成了公眾的負面人物，我甚至想要離開矽谷。但是漸漸地，我發現自己還是喜歡原來的行當，在蘋果經歷的事情絲毫沒有改變我的興趣所在。我被否定了，可是我還是愛做那些事情，所以我決定從頭再來。

當時沒覺得，但是現在看來，被蘋果開除，是我所經歷過最好的事情。成功的沉重被從頭來過的輕鬆所取代，每件事情都不那麼確定，這讓我自由地進入這輩子最有創意的時期。接下來的五年內，我開了一家叫NeXT的公司，又開了一家叫Pixar的公司，也跟後來的妻子談起了戀愛。Pixar接著製作了世界上第一部全電腦動畫電影《玩具總動員》，現在它是世界上最成功的動畫製作公司。之後，機緣巧合，蘋果電腦買下了NeXT，我又回到了蘋果，我們在NeXT開發的技術成了蘋果後來復興的核心。我也有了個和美的家庭。我很確定，如果當年蘋果沒開除我，就不會發生這些事情。這帖藥很苦口，可是我想病人需要的正是這帖藥。有時候，人生會用磚頭打你的頭。不要喪失信心。我確信，我愛我所做的事情，這就是這些年來讓我繼續走下去的唯一理由。你得找出你愛的，工作上是如此，愛情也是如此。

你的工作將填滿你人生的一大塊，唯一獲得真正滿足的方法就是做你相信是偉大的工作，而做偉大工作的唯一方法是愛你所做的事。如果你還沒找到，繼續找，別停頓。全心全力去找，你知道你一定會找到。而且，如同任何偉大的關係，情況只會隨著時間愈來愈好。所以，在你找到之前，繼續找，別停頓。

我的第三個故事，關於死亡。

我十七歲時，我讀到一則格言，好像是「把每一天都當成生命中的最後一天，你就會輕鬆自在。」它對我影響深遠，在過去33年裡，我每天早上都會照鏡子，自問：「如果今天是此生最後一天，我會做今天準備要做的事情嗎？」每當我連續多天都得到一個「不」的答案時，我就知道我必須有所改變了。提醒自己快死了，是我在人生中做出重大決定時，所用過最重要的工具。因為幾乎每件事——所有外界期望、所有名譽、所有對困窘或失敗的恐懼——在面對死亡時，都消失了，只有最重要的東西才會留下。提醒自己快死了，是我所知道的避免掉入總覺得自己會失去什麼的陷阱裡的最好方法。

人生不帶來，死不帶去，沒什麼道理不順心而為。

一年前，我被診斷出癌症。我在早上七點半做斷層掃描，在胰臟清楚地出現一個腫瘤，可我連胰臟是什麼都不知道。醫生告訴我，幾乎可以確定是不治之症，我大概只能活三到六個月了。醫生建議我回家好好跟親人們聚一聚，一種醫生對臨終病人的標準建議。意思是你得試著在幾個月內把你未來十年想跟小孩講的話講完；你得把每件事情搞定，儘量讓家人不那麼難過；你得跟人們說再見了。我整天想著那個診斷結果，那天晚上又做了一次切片，從喉嚨伸入一個內視鏡，通過胃進入腸子，插了根針進胰臟，取了一些腫瘤細胞出來。我打了鎮靜劑，不省人事，但是我老婆在場。她後來跟我說，當醫生們用顯微鏡看過那些細胞後都哭了，因為那是一種非常少見的胰臟癌，可以用手術治好。所以我接受了手術，康復了。

這是我最接近死亡的時候，我希望那會繼續是未來幾十年內最接近的一次。經歷此事後，我可以比之前死亡只是抽象概念時要更肯定地告訴你們下面這些：

沒有人想死。即使那些想上天堂的人，也想活著上天堂。但是死亡是我們共有的目的地，沒有人逃得過。這是注定的，因為死亡簡直就是生命中最棒的發明，是生命變化的媒介，送走老人們，給新生代留下空間。現在你們是新生代，但是不久的將來，你們也會逐漸變老，被送出人生的舞臺。抱歉講得這麼戲劇化，但是這是事實。

你們的時間有限，所以不要浪費時間活在別人的生活裡。不要被信條所惑——盲從信條就是活在別人思考的結果裡。不要讓別人的意見淹沒了你的心聲。最重要的是擁有追隨內心與直覺的勇氣，你的內心與直覺多少已經知道你真正想要成為什麼樣的人。任何其他事物都是次要的。

我年輕時，有本神奇的雜誌叫做《Whole Earth Catalog》，當年我們很迷這本雜誌。那是一位住在離這兒不遠的Menlo Park的Stewart Brand創辦的，他把雜誌辦得很有詩意。那是六十年代末期，個人電腦跟桌面出版還沒發明，所有內容都是打字機、剪刀跟拍立得相機做出來的。雜誌內容有點像印在紙上的Google，在Google出現之前35年就有了：很理想化，充滿新奇的工具與神奇的註記。

Stewart跟他的出版團隊出了好幾期《Whole Earth Catalog》，然後出了停刊號。當時是七十年代中期，我正是你們現在這個年齡的時候。在停刊號的封底，有張早晨鄉間小路的照片，那種你去爬山時會經過的鄉間小路。在照片下有行小字：求知若饑，虛心若愚。那是他們親筆寫下的告別訊息，我總是以此自許。在你們畢業，即將展開新生活的時候，我也以此期許你們。

求知若饑，虛心若愚。

謝謝大家。

附錄三 散文名篇

一、《青春》

Youth

Samuel Ullman

（塞繆爾· 厄爾曼，1840—1924）

Youth is not a time of life; it is a state of mind.

It is not a matter of rosy cheeks, red lips and supple knees;

It is a matter of the will, a quality of the imagination, a vigor of the emotions;

It is the freshness of the deep springs of life.

Youth means a temperamental predominance of courage over timidity,

of the appetite for adventure over the love of ease.

This often exits in a man of 60 more than a boy of 20.

Nobody grows old merely by a number of years; we grow old by deserting our ideals.

Years may wrinkle the skin, but to give up enthusiasm wrinkles the soul.

Worry, fear, self-distrust bows the heart and turns the spirit back to dust.

Whether 60 or 16, there is in every human being's heart the lure of wonder,

the unfailing childlike appetite of what's next and the joy of the game of living.

In the center of your heart and my heart there is a wireless station;

so long as it receives messages of beauty, hope, cheer, courage and power from men and from the infinite,

so long as you are young.

When the aerials are down, and your spirit is covered with snows of cynicism and the ice of pessimism,

then you are grown old, even at 20, but as long as your aerials are up,

to catch waves of optimism, there's hope you may die young at 80.

【中文譯文】

青春不是年華，而是心境；青春不是桃面、丹唇、柔膝，而是深沉的意志，恢弘的想像，熾熱的感情；青春是生命的源泉在不息湧流。

青春氣貫長虹，勇銳蓋過怯懦，進取壓倒苟安。如此銳氣，弱冠後生有之，耳順之年，則亦多見，年歲有加，並非垂老；理想丟棄，方墮暮年。

歲月悠悠，衰萎只及肌膚，熱忱拋卻，頹唐必至靈魂。憂煩，惶恐，喪失自信，定使心靈扭曲，意氣如灰。

無論年屆古稀，抑或二八芳齡，心中皆有生命之歡樂，奇蹟之誘惑，孩童般天真久盛不衰。人人心中皆深植一片追求，只要你從天上，人間追求美好，希望，歡樂，勇氣和力量，你就青春永駐，風華常存。

一旦追求消失，銳氣如同冰雪覆蓋，玩世不恭，自暴自棄油然而生，即使年方二十，實已老矣。然堅持追求，你就有望在百歲高齡告別塵寰時仍覺年青。

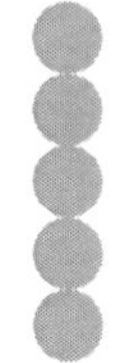

二、《論讀書》

Of Studies

Francis Bacon

（法蘭西斯· 培根，1561—1626）

Studies serve for delight, for ornament, and for ability. Their chief use for delight, is in privateness and retiring; for ornament, is in discourse; and for ability, is in the judgment, and disposition of business. For expert men can execute, and perhaps judge of particulars, one by one; but the general counsels, and the plots and marshalling of affairs, come best, from those that are learned. To spend too much time in studies is sloth; to use them too much for ornament, is affectation; to make judgment wholly by their rules, is the humor of a scholar. They perfect nature, and are perfected by experience: for natural abilities are like natural plants, that need proyning, by study; and studies themselves, do give forth directions too much at large, except they be bounded in by experience. Crafty men contemn studies, simple men admire them, and wise men use them; for they teach not their own use; but that is a wisdom without them, and above them, won by observation. Read not to contradict and confute; nor to believe and take for granted; nor to find talk and discourse; but to weigh and consider. Some books are to be tasted, others to be swallowed, and some few to be chewed and digested; that is, some books are to be read only in parts; others to be read, but not curiously; and some few to be read wholly, and with diligence and attention. Some books also may be read by deputy, and extracts made of them by others; but that would be only in the less important arguments and the meaner sort of books, else distilled books are like common distilled waters, flashy things.

Reading maketh a full man; conference a ready man; and writing an exact man. And therefore, if a man write little, he had need have a great memory; if he confer little, he had need have a present wit: and if he read little, he had need have much cunning, to seem to know, that he doth not. Histories make men wise; poets witty; the mathematics subtle; natural philosophy deep; moral grave; logic and rhetoric able to contend. Abeunt studia in mores. Nay, there is no stand or impediment in the wit, but may be wrought out by fit studies; like as diseases of the body, may have appropriate exercises. Bowling is good for the stone and reins; shooting for the lungs and breast; gentle walking for the stomach; riding for the head; and the like. So if a man's wit be wandering, let him study the mathematics; for in demonstrations, if his wit be called away never so little, he must begin again. If his wit be not apt to distinguish or find differences, let him study the Schoolmen; for they are cymini sectores. If he be not apt to beat over matters, and to call up one thing to prove and illustrate another, let him study the lawyers' cases. So every defect of the mind may have a special receipt.

【中文譯文】

讀書足以怡情，足以博彩，足以長才。其怡情也，最見於獨處幽居之時；其博彩也，最見於高談闊論之中；其長才也，最見於處世判事之際。練達之士雖能分別處理細事或一一判別枝節，然縱觀統籌、全局策劃，則捨好學深思者莫屬。讀書費時過多易惰，文采藻飾太盛則矯，全憑條文斷事乃學究故態。讀書補天然之不足，經驗又補讀書之不足，蓋天生才幹猶如自然花草，讀書然後知如何修剪移接；而書中所示，如不以經驗範之，則又大而無當。有一技之長者鄙讀書，無知者羨讀書，唯明智之士用讀書，然書並不以用處告人，用書之智不在書中，而在書外，全憑觀察得之。讀書時不可存心詰難作者，不可盡信書上所言，亦不可只為尋章摘句，而應推敲細思。書有可淺嚐者，有可吞食者，少數則需咀嚼消化。換言之，有只需讀其部分者，有只需大體涉獵者，少數則需全讀，讀時須全神貫注，孜孜不倦。書亦可請人代讀，取其所作摘要，但只限題材較次或價值不高者，否則書經提煉猶如水經蒸餾，淡而無味矣。

讀書使人充實，討論使人機智，筆記使人準確。因此不常做筆記者須記憶特強，不常討論者須天生聰穎，不常讀書者須欺世有術，始能無知而顯有知。讀史使人明智，讀詩使人靈秀，數學使人周密，科學使人深刻，倫理學使人莊重，邏輯修辭之學使人善辯：凡有所學，皆成性格。人之才智但有滯礙，無不可讀適當

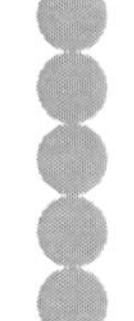

之書使之順暢，一如身體百病，皆可借相宜之運動除之。滾球利睾腎，射箭利胸肺，慢步利腸胃，騎術利頭腦，諸如此類。如智力不集中，可令讀數學，蓋演題須全神貫注，稍有分散即須重演；如不能辨異，可令讀經院哲學，蓋是輩皆吹毛求疵之人；如不善求同，不善以一物闡證另一物，可令讀律師之案卷。如此頭腦中凡有缺陷，皆有特藥可醫。

（王佐良 譯）

三、《假如給我三天光明》（節選）

Three Days to See （Excerpts）

Helen Keller

（海倫· 凱勒，1880—1968）

All of us have read thrilling stories in which the hero had only a limited and specified time to live. Sometimes it was as long as a year, sometimes as short as 24 hours. But always we were interested in discovering just how the doomed man chose to spend his last days or his last hours. I speak, of course, of free men who have a choice, not condemned criminals whose sphere of activities is strictly delimited.

Such stories set us thinking, wondering what we should do under similar circumstances. What events, what experiences, and what associations should we crowd into those last hours as mortal beings? What happiness should we find in reviewing the past? What regrets?

Sometimes I have thought it would be an excellent rule to live each day as if we should die tomorrow. Such an attitude would emphasize sharply the values of life. We should live each day with a gentleness, a vigor and a keenness of appreciation which are often lost when time stretches before us in the constant panorama of more days and months and years to come. There are those, of course, who would adopt the Epicurean motto of "Eat, drink, and be merry". But most people would be chastened by the certainty of impending death.

In stories the doomed hero is usually saved at the last minute by some stroke of fortune, but almost always his sense of values is changed. He becomes more appreciative of the meaning of life and its permanent spiritual values. It has often been noted that those who live, or have lived, in the shadow of death bring a mellow sweetness to everything they do.

Most of us, however, take life for granted. We know that one day we must die, but usually we picture that day as far in the future. When we are in buoyant health, death is all but unimaginable. We seldom think of it. The days stretch out in an endless vista. So we go about our petty tasks, hardly aware of our listless attitude toward life.

The same lethargy, I am afraid, characterizes the use of all our faculties and senses. Only the deaf appreciate hearing, only the blind realize the manifold blessings that lie in sight. Particularly does this observation apply to those who have lost sight and hearing in adult life? But those who have never suffered impairment of sight or hearing seldom make the fullest use of these blessed faculties. Their eyes and ears take in all sights and sounds hazily, without concentration and with little appreciation. It is the same old story of not being grateful for what we have until we lose it, of not being conscious of health until we are ill.

I have often thought it would be a blessing if each human being were stricken blind and deaf for a few days at some time during his early adult life. Darkness would make him more appreciative of sight; silence would teach him the joys of sound.

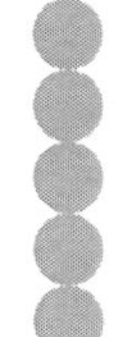

【中文譯文】

我們都讀過震撼人心的故事，故事中的主人翁只能再活一段很有限的時光，有的長達一年，有的卻短至一日。但我們總是想要知道，註定要離世的人會選擇如何度過自己最後的時光。當然，我説的是那些有選擇權利的自由人，而不是那些活動範圍受到嚴格限定的囚犯。

這樣的故事讓我們思考，在類似的處境下，我們該做些什麼？作為終有一死的人，在臨終前的幾個小時內我們應該做什麼事，經歷些什麼或做哪些聯想？回憶往昔，什麼使我們開心快樂？什麼又使我們悔恨不已？

有時我想，把每天都當做生命中的最後一天來過，也不失為一個極好的生活法則。這種態度會使人特別重視生命的價值。我們每天都應該以優雅的姿態，充沛的精力，抱著感恩之心來生活。但當時間以無休止的日、月和年在我們面前流逝時，我們卻常常沒有了這種感覺。當然，也有人奉行「吃，喝，享受」的享樂主義信條，但絕大多數人還是會被必然將會到來的死亡所折磨。

在故事中，將死的主人翁通常都在最後一刻因突降的幸運而獲救，但他的價值觀通常都會改變，他變得更加理解生命的意義及其永恆的精神價值。我們常常注意到，那些生活在或曾經生活在死亡陰影下的人無論做什麼都會感到幸福。

然而，我們中的大多數人都把生命看成是理所當然的。我們知道有一天我們必將面對死亡，但總認為那一天還在遙遠的將來。當我們身強體健之時，死亡簡直不可想像，我們很少考慮到它。日子多得好像沒有盡頭。因此我們一味忙於瑣事，幾乎意識不到我們對待生活的冷漠態度。

我擔心同樣的冷漠也存在於我們對自己官能和意識的運用上。只有聾子才理解聽力的重要，只有盲人才明白視覺的可貴，這尤其適用於那些成年後才失去視力或聽力的人。而從未遭遇視覺或聽覺損傷之苦的人很少充分利用這些寶貴的能力。他們的眼睛和耳朵模糊地感受著周圍的景物與聲音，心不在焉，也無所感激。這正像我們只有在失去後才懂得珍惜一樣，我們只有在生病後才意識到健康的可貴。

我經常想，如果每個人在年輕的時候都有幾天失明失聰，也不失為一件幸事。黑暗將使他更加感雷射明，寂靜將告訴他聲音的美妙。

四、《如果我休息，我就會生鏽》

If I Rest, I Rust

Orison Marden

（奧里森· 馬登，1850—1924）

The significant inscription found on an old key — "If I rest, I rust" — would be an excellent motto for those who are afflicted with the slightest bit of idleness. Even the most industrious person might adopt it with advantage to serve as a reminder that, if one allows his faculties to rest, like the iron in the unused key, they will soon show signs of rust and, ultimately, cannot do the work required of them.

Those who would attain the heights reached and kept by great men must keep their faculties polished by constant use, so that they may unlock the doors of knowledge, the gates that guard the entrances to the professions, to science, art, literature, agriculture — every department of human endeavor.

Industry keeps bright the key that opens the treasury of achievement. If Hugh Miller, after toiling all day in a quarry, had devoted his evenings to rest and recreation, he would never have become a famous geologist. The celebrated mathematician, Edmund Stone, would never have published a mathematical dictionary, never have found the key to science of mathematics, if he had given his spare moments to idleness. Had the little Scotch lad, Ferguson, allowed the busy brain to go to sleep while he tended sheep on the hillside instead of calculating the position of the stars by a string of beads, he would never have become a famous astronomer.

Labor vanquishes all — not inconstant, spasmodic, or ill-directed labor; but faithful, unremitting, daily effort toward a well-directed purpose. Just as truly as eternal vigilance is the price of liberty, so is eternal industry the price of noble and enduring success.

【中文譯文】

在一把舊鑰匙上發現了一則意義深遠的銘文——如果我休息，我就會生鏽。對於那些為懶散而煩惱的人來說，這將是至理名言。甚至最為勤勉的人也可以此作為警示：如果一個人有才能而不用，就像廢棄鑰匙上的鐵一樣，這些才能就會很快生鏽，並最終無法完成安排給自己的工作。

有些人想取得偉人所獲得並保持的成就，他們就必須不斷運用自身才能，以便開啟知識的大門，即那些通往人類努力探求的各個領域的大門，這些領域包括科學、藝術、文學和農業等。

勤奮使開啟成功寶庫的鑰匙保持光亮。如果休· 米勒在採石場勞作一天後，把晚上的時光用來休息消遣的話，他就不會成為名垂青史的地質學家。著名數學家愛德蒙· 斯通如果閒暇時無所事事，就不會出版數學詞典，也不會發現開啟數學之門的鑰匙。如果蘇格蘭青年弗格森在山坡上放羊時，讓他那思維活躍的大腦處於休息狀態，而不是借助一串珠子計算星星的位置，他就不會成為著名的天文學家。

勞動征服一切。這裡所指的勞動不是斷斷續續的、間歇性的或方向偏差的勞動，而是堅定的、不懈的，方向正確的每日勞動。正如要想擁有自由就要時刻保持警惕一樣，要想取得偉大的、持久的成功，就必須堅持不懈地努力。

附錄四 練習答案

第一章 人物篇

1.A—c，B—j，C—f，D—h，E—a，F—b，G—i，H—g，I—d，J—e

2.（1） To survive in prison, one must develop ways to take satisfaction in one's daily life.

（2） The authorities didn't regret giving permission, for once the garden began to flourish, I often provided the warders with some of my best tomatoes and onions.

（3） To plant a seed, watch it grow, to tend it and harvest it, offered a simple but enduring satisfaction.

（4） While I've always enjoyed gardening, it was not until I was behind bars that I was able to tend my own garden.

（5） I did not have many of the materials that the books discussed, but I learned through trial and error.

3.（1） The free time offered me an opportunity to engage in what I was interested in on Rodden Island.

（2） Because I was entitled to tending the garden of my own, I felt free from restriction.

（3） I felt liberated from the end of the forced labor.

（4） I do not know how she understood the letter.

（5） The plants grew badly at first, but they got better before long.

4.（1） enjoyed，（2） bars，（3） tend，（4） manual，（5） professors'，（6） contact，（7） alternative，（8） order，（9） techniques，（10） materials，（11） error，（12） attempted，（13） failures，（14） control，（15） harvest，（16） enduring，（17） sense，（18） owner，（19） offered，（20） freedom

5.CDAAD DBDAA

6.ADDC

第二章 經濟篇

1.A.a double-edged sword

B.the national sovereignty

C.the trade negotiation

D.an economic entity

E.inept policies

F.lopsided trade flows

G.organization of economic cooperation and development

H.boom-bust cycles

I.an ensuing financial crisis

2.（1） At the edge of a new century, globalization is a double-edged sword.

（2） In some respects, globalization is merely a trendy word for an old process.

（3） The Cold War, from the late 1940s through the 1980s, caused the United States to champion trade liberalization and economic growth as a way of combating communism.

（4） After the two world wars, Europeans saw economic unification as an antidote to deadly nationalism.

（5） Globalization continues its process but also departs from it in at least one critical respect.

3.（1） Ten years later, even after Asia's financial crisis of 1997-1998, private capital flows are still greater in number than governmental capital flows.

（2） The only difference between the recent takeover struggle between British and German radio giants and other cases is that this takeover is much bigger and a lot more bitter.

（3） Meanwhile, Latin America and sub-Saharan Africa, whose integration with the world economy has been late and limited, were not so lucky.

（4） The Asian financial crisis brought these two questions to people's attention.

（5） It was the surprisingly vigorous growth of the U.S.economy that saved the Asian crisis from escalating into an all-around economic depression.

4.（1）spontaneous，（2）communications，（3）inevitable，（4）irreversible，（5）shield，（6）imports，（7） discriminate，（8） investors，（9） matter，（10） capital，（11） productive，（12） precisely，（13）persuaded，（14）Judged，（15）backlash，（16）unpredictable，（17）recession，（18）chasing，（19）plausible，（20）constituents

5.DDAAC ADACB

6.ADB

第三章 法律篇

1.A—f，B—e，C—d，D—c，E—b，F—a

2.（1） If we don't understand this, we shall commit the gravest mistakes.

（2） He was committed to the care of an aunt.

（3） Nobody committed themselves to a definite answer.

（4） We have committed ourselves to helping them.

（5） He doubts the truth of your story but is open to conviction.

（6） I am in the full conviction (I have a firm conviction) that the situation will improve.

（7） His argument carries little conviction to Western readers.

3.（1） Each year almost a third of the people in America suffer from rough physical treatment or experience their property's being stolen.

（2） This is why when the crime rate is increasing, some crimes are not punished, or even though we punish the crimes, we do not punish them severely as we did before.

（3） Ten years' careful research has been unable to offer clear and persuading proof to show that the use of punishment leads to less crime.

（4） While the best colleges and universities admit outstanding students, some of the prisons for the most dangerous criminals now only accept criminals who have committed five serious crimes before they are put into the correctional program.

（5） The first-year cost to carry out longer prison sentences would be $150,000 to prevent one crime, and this cost is worthwhile if it is used to save your or my life, but this cost is much too high to carry out such a policy throughout the country.

4.（1） statistics，（2） illustrate，（3） committed，（4） prosecuted，（5） dismissed，（6） supervision，（7）maximum，（8）inmate，（9）released，（10）parole

5.CDDCB DBDAB

6.DCBAC

第四章 教育篇

1.A—i，B—f，C—g，D—e，E—d，F—a，G—c，H—b，I—h

2.（1） In those respects, my education had been more than adequate.

（2） It was important to respect these differences, certainly, but to stop there was like clearing the ground without any idea of what was to be built on.

（3） That was at a time when we though of other places and peoples largely out of curiosity in terms of unusual vacations.

（4） Then overnight came the great compression. Far-flung areas which had been secure in their remoteness suddenly became crowded together in a single arena.

（5） The old emphasis upon superficial differences had to give way to education for mutuality and for citizenship in the human community.

3.（1） The differences became so insignificant compared with the similarities that they were almost completely pushed aside and forgotten.

（2） The author thinks that nationalism is merely an enlarged form of tribalism.

（3） If we take away one of these things the unity of human needs will be destroyed and the human race would also perish.

（4） Here the word "engines" is used figuratively to stand for all the technological developments human beings have achieved. Human beings have invented a great many things to give us more power and to make our life easier. But these human creations are now threatening to change the balance of our environmental conditions.

（5） The author here is not talking about economic, political, or military leadership. He is talking about moral or spiritual leadership, thus "leadership of a higher level".

4.（1） that，（2） hold，（3） occurrence，（4） galaxies，（5） occupy，（6） occurs，（7） millions，（8）countless，（9） species，（10） possess，（11） combination，（12） supreme，（13） gifts，（14） intelligence，（15） foresee，（16） take，（17） visualize，（18） which，（19） conscience，（20）kinship

5.CCDBD BDDCB

6.CAA

第五章 宗教篇

1.A—e，B—d，C—c，D—b，E—a，F—f

2.（1） Her voice drifted in the crisp air like sweet crystal sugar melting slowly.

（2） Those leaves reach rather high above the water surface, like the skirts of dancing girls in all their grace.

（3） Long live peace!

（4） There goes the bell!

（5） From the window came sound of music.

（6） Never in my life have I seen such a thing.

3.（1） When I say the year I got Maheegun was the happiest (year) of my life, I don't mean that Maheegun never caused troubles.

（2） By that time, it was snowing heavily, and the air was so thick with big snowflakes that I couldn't see through them, but I realized that I had taken the wrong direction, for there was no creek when I came last time.

（3） I knew that it was dangerous to move on in the blinding snow, and that the only thing to do was to stay where I was and get some sleep during the night and hope that I would find the snowstorm had stopped the next morning.

（4） As I had lost a lot of blood, and it was extremely cold, I was sick and weak.

4.（1） hunting，（2） about，（3） games，（4） grown，（5） handsome，（6） mantle，（7） happiest，（8）myself，（9）bushes，（10） paws

5.AABBD ACBBC

6.CACAAB

第六章 環保篇

1.（1） to delight one's eye

（2） lethal weapons

（3） to invade one's privacy

（4） intensification of agriculture

（5） modify the tone

（6） natural reserves

（7） air contamination

（8） introduced species

（9） to work miracles

（10） to restrain impulse

2.（1） In autumn, oak, maple and birch set up a blaze of color that flamed and flickered across a background of pines.

（2） The roadsides, once so attractive, were now lined with browned and withered vegetation as though swept by fire.

（3） No witchcraft, no enemy action had silenced the rebirth of new life in this stricken world. The people had done it themselves.

（4） What has already silenced the voices of spring in countless towns in America? This book is an attempt to explain.

（5） It is not my contention that chemical insecticides must never be used. I do contend that we have put poisonous and biologically potent chemicals indiscriminately into the hands of persons largely or wholly ignorant of their potentials for harm.

3.（1） Then, as if by some evil power, disaster struck the community: strange diseases quickly struck down large numbers of chicken; the cattle and sheep became ill and died.

（2） The physical features and habits of the living things on earth have been shaped by their surroundings.

（3） Man is changing the nature of the world rapidly while nature adjusts to the changes slowly. Therefore adjustment can never keep up with change, and a new balance between living things and their environment can hardly be reached.Antithesis is used here.

（4） The more insecticides are sprayed, the less effective they will become in destroying the pests. The more deadly chemicals will be developed to kill them. This process will go on endlessly.

（5） By spraying insecticides on food grains, vegetables and fruit, we have caused large numbers of people to absorb harmful chemicals without asking whether they would like to do so and often without their knowing it.

4.（1）contention，（2）contend，（3）potent，（4）ignorant，（5）

potentials，（6）contact，（7）consent，（8）investigation，（9）wildlife，（10）concern

5.CBCBD ABDDB

6.BBDC

第七章 文學篇

1.A—c，B—k，C—h，D—i，E—e，F—l，G—b，H—g，I—f，J—j，K—a，L—d，M—n，N—o，O—m

2.（1） New as I was to the faculty, I could have told this specimen a number of things.

（2） Will you be presiding over a family that maintains some contact with the great democratic intellect? Will there be a book in the house? Will there be a painting a reasonable sensitive man can look without shuddering? Will the kids ever get to hear Bach?

（3） If you are too much in a hurry, or too arrogantly proud of your own limitations, to accept as a gift to your humanity some pieces of the minds of Aristotle, or Chaucer, or Einstein, you are neither a developed human nor a useful citizen of a democracy.

（4） For a great book is necessarily a gift; it offers you a life you have not the time to live yourself, and it takes you into a world you have not the time to travel in literal time.

（5） When I say that a university has no real existence and no real purpose except as it succeeds in putting you in touch, both as specialists and as humans, with those human minds your human minds needs to include.

3.（1） The B. S. certificate would be an official proof that the holder had special knowledge of pharmacy, but it would also be a proof that he/she had learned some profound ideas of the past.

（2） You have to take responsibility for the work you do. If you are a pharmacist, you should make sure that aspirin is not mixed with poisonous chemicals. As an engineer, you shouldn't get things out of control. If you become a lawyer, you should make sure an innocent person is not sentenced to death because you lack adequate legal knowledge and skill to defend your client.

（3） If you don't want to improve your mind and broaden your horizon by studying a little literature, philosophy and the fine arts and history, you shouldn't be studying here at college.

（4） You will become an uneducated, ignorant person who can only work machines and operate mechanical equipment.

（5） A number of such push-button savages get college degrees. We cannot help that. But even with their degree, we can't say that these people have received a proper college education. It is more accurate to say that they come through college without learning anything.

4.（1） techniques，（2） technical，（3） stored，（4） peculiar，（5） accomplishment，（6） acquire，（7）fragments，（8） Virgil，（9） Dante，（10） Shakespeare，（11） liberal，（12） specialized，（13）existence，（14） succeeds，（15） touch，（16） specialists，（17） include，（18） by，（19）existence，（20） implicitly，（21） aided，（22） attempt，（23） storehouse，（24）available，（25）expertise

5.ADCAB AABCA

6.DABBD

第八章 奧運篇

1.A： ADACD

B： CBDB

一生必知的世界文化（英語導覽）：名人故事 × 經濟策略 × 文學名著 × 法律思潮，一本書帶你從八個層面全方位掌握英語

編　　著：莊琦春，陸香，丁碩瑞
發 行 人：黃振庭
出 版 者：崧燁文化事業有限公司
發 行 者：崧燁文化事業有限公司
E-mail：sonbookservice@gmail.com
粉 絲 頁：https://www.facebook.com/sonbookss/
網　　址：https://sonbook.net/
地　　址：台北市中正區重慶南路一段六十一號八樓 815 室
Rm. 815, 8F., No.61, Sec. 1, Chongqing S. Rd., Zhongzheng Dist., Taipei City 100, Taiwan
電　　話：(02)2370-3310
傳　　真：(02)2388-1990
印　　刷：京峯彩色印刷有限公司（京峰數位）
律師顧問：廣華律師事務所 張珮琦律師

定　　價：299 元
發行日期：2022 年 09 月修訂一版
◎本書以 POD 印製

國家圖書館出版品預行編目資料

一生必知的世界文化（英語導覽）：名人故事 × 經濟策略 × 文學名著 × 法律思潮，一本書帶你從八個層面全方位掌握英語 / 莊琦春，陸香，丁碩瑞編著 . -- 修訂一版 . -- 臺北市：崧燁文化事業有限公司，2022.09
面；　公分
POD 版
ISBN 978-626-332-652-1(平裝)
1.CST: 英語 2.CST: 讀本
805.18　　　　11101238

電子書購買

臉書